ARCHES AND CANYONLANDS NATIONAL PARKS

In the Land of Standing Rocks

Adventures with the Parkers

Mike Graf

ILLUSTRATED BY
Marjorie Leggitt

FALCONGUIDES

GUILFORD, CONNECTICUT
HELENA, MONTANA
AN IMPRINT OF GLOBE PEQUOT

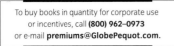
FALCONGUIDES®

Text © 2013 Mike Graf
Illustrations © 2013 Marjorie Leggitt

FalconGuides is an imprint of Globe Pequot Press.
Falcon, FalconGuides, and Outfit Your Mind are registered trademarks of Morris Book Publishing, LLC.

Illustrations by Marjorie Leggitt
Models for twins: Amanda and Ben Frazier

Photos by Mike Graf with the following exceptions, which are licensed by Shutterstock .com: inside front cover, pp. i, 8, 22, 38 © Darren J. Bradley; p. i inset, p. 110, inside back cover © Keneva Photography; p. 1 © Peter Wey; pp. 7, 55, 59 Courtesy National Park Service; p. 11 © Scott Prokop; pp. 14, 17 (bottom) © Rudy Balasko; p. 17 (top) © Jeffrey M. Frank; p. 19 © Erik Harrison; p. 25 © Mountain Photography and Software LLC; p. 26 © Patricia Hofmeester; p. 27 © Manamana; p. 42 © fotokik_dot_com; p. 69 © RIRF Stock; pp. 71 (top), 73 © J. Norman Reid; p. 82 © Dennis Donohue; pp. 101, 105, 106 © Robert Crum; p. 109 © Boris15

Maps courtesy of National Park Service

Layout: Melissa Evarts
Project editor: Julie Marsh

Library of Congress Cataloging-in-Publication Data

Graf, Mike.
  Arches and Canyonlands national parks : in the land of standing rocks / Mike Graf, illustrated by Marjorie Leggitt.
    p. cm. — (Adventures with the Parkers)
  ISBN 978-0-7627-7962-8
  1. Arches National Park (Utah)—Guidebooks—Juvenile literature. 2. Canyonlands National Park (Utah)—Guidebooks—Juvenile literature. I. Leggitt, Marjorie C., ill. II. Title.
  F832.A7G73 2012
  979.2'58—dc23
                                                            2012012734

Printed in the United States of America
10 9 8 7 6 5 4 3 2 1

A First-Time Leftie

James put down his pen and looked at his family. His twin sister, Morgan, and his mom and dad were staring out at the vast, dry landscape surrounding their campsite in eastern Nevada, on their way to Arches and Canyonlands National Parks. After a few moments, Mom gathered cooking supplies and put them on the picnic table.

James picked up and dropped his pen, twice. Then he noisily cleared his throat.

Dad noticed the cue. "Have you got something there for us?"

"Only the start of a story I'm working on," James replied. "But I like what I've written so far."

"Will you read it to us?" Mom asked curiously.

"Sure," James replied. "It's about John Wesley Powell. Since I did that report last year on his expeditions, I can't stop thinking about his travels."

For a moment James's mind drifted back to spring semester in Mr. Block's class. "And my family is going to the area Powell explored this summer," James informed his teacher at the end of his speech.

"That was a great presentation, James," Mr. Block said. "Can you come back next fall and tell me how your travels went?"

"Sure," James said, before receiving a round of applause and then taking his seat.

Morgan scooted next to her brother. "Go ahead," she said, while nudging James and glancing at his journal. "I want to hear your story too."

James quickly looked over his writing. Then he began. "The first line is actually something Powell said."

The landscape everywhere away from the river is rock, cliffs of rock, tables of rock, plateaus of rock, terraces of rock, crags of rock . . .

James paused for a second and looked up.

"Wow," Dad pondered. "It must have been something to come upon the area back then. Southeast Utah is definitely a unique part of the country."

Morgan glanced at James's story. "How come your writing's so sloppy?"

"I'm using my left hand," James replied nonchalantly.

"Left hand?" Mom echoed. "Why?"

James paused for a second, thinking, then answered. "Because after the Civil War, that's all John Wesley Powell had."

"Interesting," Dad replied. "Go on. I want to hear more."

"I'm writing this now as if he's reporting in his journal," James explained.

"That's unique and creative," Mom said. "I like that approach."

Encouraged, James continued.

June 24th, 1869

We've been traveling for about a month now along the placid Green River. The crew is famished, but we've been finding some game along the way. Of course we have plenty of water, but it's muddy and I don't think it's settling well in our stomachs.

The whole region is amazing. The rock formations are different than anything any of us have ever seen. Outside of that there's not much life out here (although the crew thinks there might still be some Indians around).

Several of the gang are grumbling about quitting. After Disaster Falls when we lost so much of our equipment and food, I can understand why. A few have commented that this whole journey is just a waste of time. Others are more concerned about the unknown dangers or rapids that lie ahead. But so far I've persuaded them to continue on.

We'll see how it goes.

John Wesley Powell

James put his journal down and looked at his family.

"That," Dad exclaimed, "is fantastic!"

"I definitely want to hear more," Morgan added enthusiastically.

"I'm going to work on it while we're on this trip," James replied.

Morgan took one more look at James's journal. "Not bad for a first-time leftie," she acknowledged. Then Morgan noticed the initials for the signature her brother had written at the bottom of the journal.

"JWP!" Morgan realized. "Look! John Wesley Powell and James William Parker."

"Hey!" James exclaimed. "You're right!"

Don't Forget to Brake!

The following morning the Parkers left eastern Nevada and drove across Utah. Late in the day they arrived at Moab, the gateway town to Arches and Canyonlands National Parks.

There the family stocked up on groceries and other supplies. They camped near the wide, muddy Colorado River, just outside of town.

The Parkers got up early the next day and headed toward Canyonlands' Island in the Sky district on Highway 313. As the road climbed a series of twists and turns, the family gazed at the rock-strewn scenery outside. Soon a sign along the road appeared: NO FOOD, GAS, LODGING, OR WATER AHEAD!

"I love it!" Dad exclaimed. "True wilderness in one of the least developed parts of the United States."

The road reached a plateau, and the area was now a grassy tableland. The family eventually passed a turnoff to Dead Horse Point State Park.

"You gotta love the names out here," Dad commented as he drove.

James pulled out a Canyonlands park map. He quickly scanned it. "You should hear some of the other names," he said.

"Tell us some," Mom requested.

James surveyed the map and began reading. "Well, there's Candlestick Tower, Washer Woman Arch, and Upheaval Dome," James said, studying the Island in the Sky area.

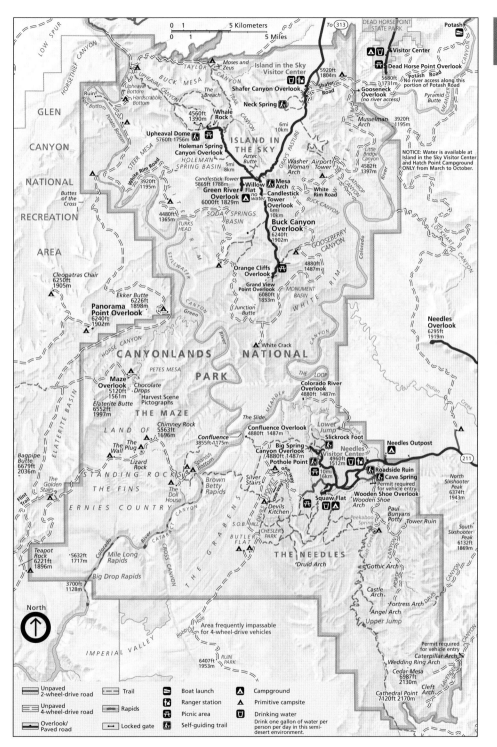

To (313)

DEAD HORSE POINT STATE PARK

Potash

Visitor Center

Dead Horse Point Overlook
5680ft
1731m

Potash Road
No river access along this
portion of Potash Road

Gooseneck
Overlook
(no river access)

Pyramid
Butte

5920ft
1804m

Shafer
Road

Island in the Sky
Visitor Center

Shafer Canyon Overlook

Neck Spring

Moses and
Zeus

TAYLOR

BUCK MESA

CANYON

The
Breach

LOW SPUR

HORSETHIEF CANYON

UPHEAVAL CANYON

Upheaval
Bottom

Hardscrabble
Bottom

Ruin

4560ft
1390m

Whale
Rock

Upheaval Dome
5760ft 1756m

Holeman Spring
Canyon Overlook

HOLEMAN
SPRING BASIN

Aztec
Butte

ISLAND IN
THE SKY

Washer
Woman
Arch

Airport
Tower

Musselman
Arch

3920ft
1195m

Little
Bridge
Canyon

LATHROP CANYON

4582ft
1397m

NOTICE: Water is available at
Island in the Sky Visitor Center
and Hatch Point Campground
ONLY from March to October.

GLEN

CANYON

NATIONAL

RECREATION

AREA

STEER MESA

White Rim Road

3920ft
1195m

4480ft
1365m

Candlestick Tower
5865ft 1788m

Green River
Overlook
6000ft 1829m

Willow
Flat
no
water

Mesa
Arch

Candlestick
Tower
Overlook

White
Rim Road

Buck Canyon
Overlook
6240ft
1902m

6mi
10km

BUCK CANYON

GOOSEBERRY CANYON

WHITE

RIM

Colorado

LOCKHART CANYON

Buttes
of the
Cross

SODA SPRINGS
BASIN

TURKS
HEAD

Cleopatras Chair
6250ft
1905m

STILLWATER

Ekker Butte
6226ft
1898m

Panorama
Point Overlook
6240ft
1902m

Orange Cliffs
Overlook

Grand View
Point Overlook
6080ft
1853m

Junction
Butte

4880ft
1487m

MONUMENT
BASIN

RIVER

Needles
Overlook
6295ft
1919m

HORSE CANYON

CANYON

Green

CANYONLANDS

NATIONAL

White Crack

PARK

PETES MESA

Maze
Overlook
5120ft
1561m

Chocolate
Drops

Harvest Scene
Pictographs

Elaterite Butte
6552ft
1997m

THE MAZE

LAND OF

Chimney Rock
5563ft
1696m

Confluence
3855ft 1175m

The Slide

Confluence Overlook
4880ft 1487m

Big Spring
Canyon Overlook
4880ft 1487m

Pothole Point

THE LOOP

MEANDER

Colorado River
Overlook
4880ft 1487m

Lower
Jump

Slickrock Foot

Needles
Visitor Center
4960ft
1512m

one
way

Salt

Indian

Creek

211

Needles Outpost

North
Sixshooter
Peak
6374ft
1943m

ELATERITE BASIN

STANDING ROCK

THE FINS

ERNIES COUNTRY

The
Plug

The
Wall

Lizard
Rock

Spanish
Bottom

Brown
Betty
Rapids

The
Doll
House

Flint
Trail

The
Golden
Stairs

Bagpipe
Butte
6679ft
2036m

Silver
Stairs

10mi
16km

Roadside Ruin

Cave Spring
Permit required
for vehicle entry

Squaw Flat

Wooden Shoe Overlook

Wooden Shoe
Arch

Devils
Kitchen

DEVILS POCKET

CHESLER
PARK

S.O.B.
HILL

Paul
Bunyans
Potty

Tower Ruin

Peekaboo
Spring

South
Sixshooter
Peak
6132ft
1869m

COLORADO

River

CATARACT CANYON

CROSS CANYON

THE GRABENS

BUTLER
FLAT

Teapot
Rock
6221ft
1896m

5632ft
1717m

Mile Long
Rapids

Big Drop Rapids

3700ft
1128m

Salt Creek

HORSE CANYON

DAVIS CANYON

THE NEEDLES

Druid Arch

Gothic Arch

Castle
Arch

Fortress Arch

Angel Arch

Upper Jump

North

Area frequently impassable
for 4-wheel-drive vehicles

Bobbys
Hole

RUIN
PARK

6407ft
1953m

IMPERIAL VALLEY

Permit required
for vehicle entry

Caterpillar Arch

Wedding Ring Arch

Cedar Mesa
6987ft
2130m

Cathedral Point
7120ft 2170m

Cleft
Arch

LAVENDER CANYON

0   1   5 Kilometers
0   1   5 Miles

Unpaved
2-wheel-drive road

Unpaved
4-wheel-drive road

Overlook/
Paved road

Trail

Rapids

Locked gate

Boat launch

Ranger station

Picnic area

Self-guiding trail

Campground

Primitive campsite

Drinking water

Drink one gallon of water per
person per day in this semi-
desert environment.

Then James searched other parts of the park. "And there's the Maze, Musselman Arch, Chocolate Drops, the Great Gallery, and Paul Bunyans Potty." James paused to laugh. "It really says that!" he exclaimed.

"It all sounds pretty intriguing," Mom said.

Soon the family crossed the Canyonlands National Park boundary. They stopped briefly at the visitor center. After that the road became a thin two-lane highway with cliffs dropping off into deep canyons on both sides. Dad maneuvered across the "Neck" and parked at the nearby Shafer Canyon overlook.

Morgan, James, Mom, and Dad piled out of the car. A sign indicated the Neck Spring Trail. "Hmm," Dad pondered. "Maybe we can do that hike later."

Morgan looked at her parents. "What do they mean by the 'Neck'?"

Mom found a sign about it and called everyone over.

The Parkers read about cattle grazing in the area and how the Neck made a natural barrier for easy corralling of cattle.

Across the parking lot two vans were surrounded by a group of people in bike shorts and colorful jerseys. Everyone started unloading mountain bikes from racks on top of the vans. Morgan watched until all the bikes were down.

The group of cyclists gathered around a leader. "Okay," she began. "We're going to drop you off here. You'll ride all the way to Potash, about the most spectacular twenty miles you'll ever bike anywhere. There'll be two rest stops along the way." The guide paused

A great way to explore the park!

to hand out maps. "And we'll have a well-earned lunch waiting for you once we meet again down by the river."

The guide looked the group over. "One more thing. Shafer Trail down into the canyon is very steep. Don't forget to use your brakes! And it's a dirt road the entire way, too. There should be no land speed records broken here."

The bikers started pedaling away. Meanwhile Morgan, James, Mom, and Dad meandered over to the lookout. They gazed out at the panorama of deep, sheer-walled canyons.

Morgan gazed down. "There's the road!" she exclaimed.

The family waited a few seconds until the bikers appeared, gliding down the steep, switchbacked descent. Some took it faster than others. "Whoo-hoo!" one rider called out, a trail of dust in her wake.

"Boy, that looks like an experience," Dad announced.

"And they'll get to see the river," Morgan added.

After a few more minutes at the overlook, the Parkers returned to their car. They drove on and stopped a short time later at the popular Mesa Arch Trail.

The family took the short walk and soon arrived at the canyon rim. Spread out before them were massive canyonlands framed by a rainbow-shaped arch at the top of the mesa.

Mesa Arch

The family approached the sandy-colored span of stone until it felt as if they got any closer, they would tumble into the desolate canyon.

"It's like a giant window into the desert," Morgan exclaimed while taking out her camera. Then she extended her arm out to pretend to touch the arch. "It seems so close."

Mom held on to Morgan's shoulder and peeked into the chasm far below. "Please don't try that anymore," she said. "It's a long way down."

Dad took a deep breath and gazed at the immense, wild scenery. "Now this is a national park!" he exclaimed.

Meanwhile, James pulled out his map and studied it while glancing up at the distant figures of rock in the canyon. "Hey," he announced. "There's also an arch way out there. And . . ." James paused to study a distant rock pillar with a hole in it. He looked at the map again. "It does kind of look like a woman bending over to do laundry."

James pointed out Washer Woman Arch to his family.

"Wow," Mom said. "We really are in an unusual place."

Ancient Food Storage

The Parkers spent the next few hours at Willow Flat Campground waiting for the heat to subside. They set up their tents and rested in the shade while a few flies and gnats buzzed around.

In the late afternoon, Dad yawned and stretched, then got out of his chair. "Okay," he called out. "Let's go explore."

The family drove a short distance to the nearby Aztec Butte trailhead.

After trudging along the sandy start of the trail, the Parkers began climbing steeply up the butte. They followed rock piles, or cairns, marking the way.

A quarter of a mile later, they made it to the flat-topped summit. Morgan, James, Mom, and Dad gazed at the views surrounding them. In the distance the massive, remote canyonlands beckoned to be explored.

Soon the trail dipped to just below the summit. Now the pathway weaved through a series of eroded alcoves and small caves. "It's so nice and cool in here," Morgan commented about being in the shade.

Suddenly the family approached a bunch of flat stones piled up to make a room at the back of a cave. "Whoa!" Mom exclaimed. "Look at that!"

"What is it?" Morgan asked, inching closer to the stone structure.

After a moment Mom answered. "I think it's a granary. It's where Native Americans stored their seeds."

"They sure knew what they were doing," Dad remarked. "Storing seeds up here where they could stay cool in the shade and out of reach of others."

Morgan took another step toward the granary. "I wonder if there's anything left in it."

Ancient food storage location

Mom held Morgan back. "I doubt it. Scavengers like rats would have gotten to it by now. And we need to leave it alone anyway. It's an important historical relic that shows how people in the past lived."

EARLY FARMERS

Around AD 950 Ancestral Puebloans moved into the Canyonlands area. They were mostly farmers and grew crops of corn, beans, and squash. They also gathered seeds. These people built granaries throughout the area for storing their corn seeds and nuts from season to season. The granaries were often in hidden or hard-to-get-to locations and had small doors that were covered with slabs of rock. This helped to keep the rodents out. The people of this region left the area in the late 1200s due to a prolonged drought. Even today some granaries still have corn cobs, seeds, and other food items in them. Recently, archaeologists have taken some of the seeds and sprouted them, eight hundred years after they were placed there by the Native Americans.

The family spent a moment longer looking at the ancient structure. Then they followed the trail under a ledge, passing more eroded caverns and another dilapidated granary.

The path returned to the summit and looped back to where they had climbed up. From there the Parkers scrambled back down the butte and returned to their car.

After a quick drive Morgan, James, Mom, and Dad arrived at the end of the road at Upheaval Dome. They hiked up another short trail and gazed at one of Canyonlands' most unusual formations, a giant crater surrounded by cliffs and partially filled with mounds of grayish rock.

"Wow," Dad commented. "That is one huge hole in the ground."

The family gathered around an information sign and read the two theories about what caused Upheaval Dome.

SALT OR METEORITE

Some scientists say Upheaval Dome was formed by salt. The area underneath Canyonlands National Park has a thick layer of salt that was left behind when the seas of the past evaporated. This salt layer has been buried under rock thousands of feet thick. Over time the weight or pressure on the salt layer caused the salt to bubble up, much like ice does in a glacier. This created the salt dome at Upheaval Dome.

Others say Upheaval Dome is the result of a large meteorite, about one-third mile in diameter, hitting the earth about sixty million years ago. The explosion from the impact created the crater, and erosion since then has washed away any of the meteorite's remains.

"Okay," James announced. "Those who think it was caused by a meteorite, stand over there."

James and Mom walked over.

"What about you two?" James asked Morgan and Dad.

"I'm not really sure," Dad replied.

"Me neither," Morgan added.

Morgan stared down into the large, circular crater with gray, sandy rock piled up in the middle.

Finally Dad remarked, "I know I sound like a broken record, but I've never seen anything quite like this place."

"I feel the same way," Morgan agreed.

The Parkers left Upheaval Dome and made one last stop before sunset. They parked at the Whale Rock trailhead and, guided by two sets of handrails, scrambled up to the massive, smooth rock's summit. There they wandered around, enjoying the views of the whole Island in the Sky area and the distant canyons as they faded into shadows from the dropping sun.

The Moab Facial

The next morning James got up before his family. During the night he had decided not to write a journal from John Wesley Powell's point of view, but to turn Powell's adventures into a story. James wrote quickly while his thoughts were fresh . . .

"So, you say you saw some man-made structures?" Captain Powell inquired of one of his younger crew members.

"Yes, sir," the young explorer reported. "We discovered what looked like a food storage area just below a cliff."

"Anything else?"

"We didn't go farther up the canyon after that."

"Could it be that there are Indians still around here?" Captain Powell mused.

"Could be. But not by the looks of what we saw. The granary hasn't been used—at least by people—in years."

Both men fell silent. They gazed downstream at the meandering river. Meanwhile the rest of the crew was taking down camp and packing the boats.

"We'll have to continue and see what lies ahead," Powell concluded. "Since we're the first known white men rafting this river, we have no idea what to expect."

James heard his family stirring inside the tent. He put down his pen and took a deep breath.

A few minutes later all the Parkers were up. They ate breakfast and packed up their camp. James stuffed his story into his backpack.

After loading the car the family drove south to the end of the road at Grand View Point. A ranger was stationed there, ready to give a talk. The Parkers joined the small audience, gazing at the remote, convoluted canyons.

"Welcome, everyone," the ranger began. "I'm Rachel. It's pretty dry out here, huh? In fact, from where we are right now, we can't see any water at all. But it's water that shaped this canyon and the entire area. It just took a little time."

Rachel explained. "Two hundred million years ago, water was everywhere around here. This whole place was like a giant mudflat. We know that by the sea fossils found in the area and the ripples in the rock." The ranger passed around a wavy piece of reddish stone.

"Sediment," Rachel went on, "was deposited here as mud from rivers.

"But about one hundred million years ago, things dried up. The continents drifted apart, causing climate change to occur, and eventually this whole region became a massive Sahara-like desert with sand dunes that were three to five hundred feet high.

Grand View Point

"In fact," Rachel continued, "we still have quite a bit of sand in this region. And when it's windy—which it often is—the sand really whips around. Sometimes the fine grains of sand can blast your face and any exposed skin. We call it the Moab Facial—although I doubt it makes any of us more attractive."

The Parkers looked at each other and chuckled.

"Anyway, the culminating event happened about fifteen million years ago. That's when a massive uplift occurred on the Colorado Plateau. This was due to the Pacific Ocean Plate colliding with the North American Plate.

"Because of the uplift the Green and Colorado Rivers started to flow faster and erode away sediment quickly. The water carved out about six thousand feet of rock, forming the canyons we see today.

"And the rivers are still eroding away soil and rock, especially during monsoon season—July and August. By the way, the name Colorado River means 'red' river. It's still full of mud today. Along with the rivers, winter frost and thaws also help to break apart the rocks.

"So," Rachel concluded, "although there's no water visible from here now, there sure was then!"

The group clapped for Rachel. After saying good-bye, the Parkers trekked out to Grand View Point.

The one-mile trail eventually led to the edge of the cliff. Along the way, Dad recalled a chapter from a book written by Edward Abbey, a former ranger at Arches National Park and famous environmental author focusing on the Desert Southwest. "He wrote about this very spot," Dad shared. "And about a man dying out here because of dehydration."

Mom glanced at the water bottle dangling from her pack.

At the end of the path, the family gazed in awe at the immense, desolate canyons sprawled in all directions.

"There's the Needles way out there," Dad gaped, pointing to the many pillars of standing rocks.

"I can see where they got their name," Morgan added.

James looked down toward the right. "And the Green River. So you can see water, at least from here!"

Morgan peeked over the immense cliff, then backed away. "A lot of good that water would do us way down there," she remarked.

Then Morgan noticed a dirt road far below. Soon a van appeared on the road, kicking up a small cloud of dust. The vehicle meandered along. "I wonder what they're doing down there." Morgan said.

"Hmm," Mom replied. "Perhaps they're exploring a remote part of the park, just like we will be doing soon."

The Parkers made one more stop in the area. They drove back along the park road to a picnic area where the short trail to the White Rim overlook began. "For more views," Mom mentioned along the way.

The mostly flat trail eventually narrowed to a jutting peninsula extending out over the canyon. Finally, at a rocky promontory, the family could go no farther. "I guess this is the end," Dad said while examining the long, steep drop-offs that surrounded them.

Mom also peeked over the edge. "I think this view is at least as good if not better than Grand View."

Morgan saw a dirt road again. "Is that road on the map, James?"

James unfolded his park map and studied it. "It must be the White Rim Road."

Then Morgan and James saw the vehicle from earlier. "There's that van!" Morgan exclaimed. "And there are people nearby with bikes."

"It seems like they're having a picnic," Dad observed. "It might be one of the outfitters leading bike tours along the White Rim Road. The Moab area is so famous for that. It's supposed to be the mountain bike capital of the world."

After staring out over the canyon for a few more minutes, the family backtracked a short distance. They sat down in the shade of a giant mushroom-shaped rock. "I think it's time for our own picnic," Mom announced.

Would You Buy That Car?

The Parkers spent another night at Willow Flat Campground. They got up before dawn the next morning, packed quickly, and headed into Arches National Park before sunrise.

The visitor center was still closed as they drove by. "It's nice that we reserved our campsite here ahead of time," Mom commented.

The road past the entrance climbed abruptly into the park. "I feel like we're on a ride at Disneyland or something," Morgan announced as they chugged along, passing the fantasyland of rocks outside.

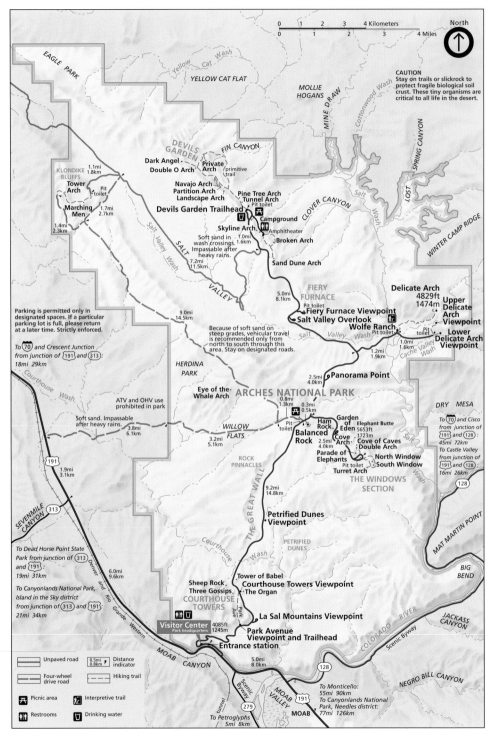

0 1 2 3 4 Kilometers
0 1 2 3 4 Miles

North

EAGLE PARK

YELLOW CAT FLAT

Yellow Cat Wash

MOLLIE
HOGANS

MINE DRAW

Cottonwood Wash

LOST SPRING CANYON

CAUTION
Stay on trails or slickrock to
protect fragile biological soil
crust. These tiny organisms are
critical to all life in the desert.

DEVILS GARDEN

FIN CANYON

Dark Angel
Double O Arch
Private
Arch
primitive
trail

KLONDIKE
BLUFFS
1.1mi
1.8km

Tower
Arch
Pit
toilet

Navajo Arch
Partition Arch
Landscape Arch

Pine Tree Arch
Tunnel Arch
Pit toilet

CLOVER CANYON

Salt Wash

WINTER CAMP RIDGE

Marching
Men
1.7mi
2.7km

Devils Garden Trailhead

Campground
Amphitheater

1.4mi
2.3km

Skyline Arch

Soft sand in
wash crossings.
Impassable after
heavy rains.
7.2mi
11.5km

1.0mi
1.6km
Broken Arch

Sand Dune Arch

SALT VALLEY

FIERY
FURNACE
5.0mi
8.1km
Pit toilet
Fiery Furnace Viewpoint
Salt Valley Overlook
Wolfe Ranch

Delicate Arch
4829ft
1474m

Upper
Delicate
Arch
Viewpoint

Lower
Delicate Arch
Viewpoint

Pit toilet

Parking is permitted only in
designated spaces. If a particular
parking lot is full, please return
at a later time. Strictly enforced.

9.0mi
14.5km

Because of soft sand on
steep grades, vehicular travel
is recommended only from
north to south through this
area. Stay on designated roads.

Salt Valley Wash

1.2mi
1.9km

1.0mi
1.6km
Cache Valley Wash

To 70 and Crescent Junction
from junction of
191 and 313:
18mi 29km

HERDINA
PARK

2.5mi
4.0km
Panorama Point

DRY MESA

ATV and OHV use
prohibited in park

Eye of the
Whale Arch

ARCHES NATIONAL PARK

0.8mi
1.3km

0.3mi
0.5km

Garden
of
Eden

Elephant Butte
5653ft
1723m

To 70 and Cisco
from junction of
191 and 128:
45mi 72km

Soft sand. Impassable
after heavy rains.
3.8mi
6.1km

WILLOW
FLATS

Pit
toilet

Ham
Rock.

Balanced
Rock

2.5mi
4.0km

Cove
Arch.

Cove of Caves
Double Arch

To Castle Valley
from junction of
191 and 128:
16mi 26km

191

1.9mi
3.1km

3.2mi
5.1km

Parade of
Elephants
Pit toilet
Turret Arch

North Window
South Window

THE WINDOWS
SECTION

128

ROCK
PINNACLES

9.2mi
14.8km

313

SEVENMILE
CANYON

Courthouse Wash

To Dead Horse Point State
Park from junction of 313
and 191:
19mi 31km

6.0mi
9.6km

Denver and Rio Grande Western

Petrified Dunes
Viewpoint

PETRIFIED
DUNES

THE GREAT WALL

MAT MARTIN POINT

BIG
BEND

To Canyonlands National
Park, Island in the Sky district
from junction of 313 and 191:
21mi 34km

Courthouse Wash

ROCK
PINNACLES

Tower of Babel
Courthouse Towers Viewpoint
The Organ

COLORADO RIVER

JACKASS
CANYON

Sheep Rock
Three Gossips
COURTHOUSE
TOWERS

La Sal Mountains Viewpoint

Scenic Byway

Visitor Center
Park headquarters
4085ft
1245m

Park Avenue
Viewpoint and Trailhead
Entrance station

MOAB CANYON

6.0mi
8.0km

128

NEGRO BILL CANYON

Scenic Byway

tunnel

279

MOAB
VALLEY

191

MOAB

To Monticello:
55mi 90km
To Canyonlands National
Park, Needles district:
77mi 124km

To Petroglyphs
5mi 8km

Legend

Unpaved road		0.5mi 0.8km	Distance indicator
Four-wheel drive road			
			Hiking trail
Picnic area			Interpretive trail
Restrooms			Drinking water

At the top of the pass, the family glimpsed the La Sal Mountains to the east. They slowly drove past the towering fins of rock at the Park Avenue trailhead. "Later we'll check that out," Dad whispered in awe.

Mom continued driving. Soon more massive rock formations, the Courthouse Towers and Three Gossips, came into view. Dad gazed at the rock monoliths. "Entrada sandstone," he mused, "sure is colorful and unique."

"And everything is so photogenic," Morgan added, trying to get a picture out the car window.

The Parkers passed petrified sand dunes to the right of the road. Mom pressed on, driving slowly, as no other cars were out this early.

Suddenly, just over a rise, a flagperson waved the family down, stopping them right on the seemingly empty highway.

"Maybe there's construction ahead," Dad suggested.

The flagperson casually walked over to the Parkers' car, and Mom rolled down the window.

Courthouse Towers

Morgan noticed a crew of people with camera equipment on a flatbed truck up ahead. Farther along was a stylish, shiny, brand-new red sports car. A family of four was seated in the car gazing out at the scenery with beaming faces. "It doesn't look like construction," Morgan said.

The flagperson approached the driver's side of the car. She leaned in toward the Parkers. "Sorry for the delay," she informed them. "It'll be just a few minutes."

"What's going on?" Mom inquired.

The flagperson answered. "You love the scenery here, right? Well so does Hollywood. They're filming a car commercial up there. But the permit issued by the park requires that they do it early in the morning before all the visitors start rolling in. There's better light for filming at this time anyway. It won't be long. They're only allowed to hold up traffic for a few minutes."

MOVIES ARE MADE HERE! The world's largest concentration of natural arches and other spectacular rock formations in southeast Utah has been the backdrop for many movies including *Thelma and Louise, Indiana Jones and the Last Crusade, City Slickers II,* and *Mission Impossible II,* as well as dozens of commercials and music videos.

The Parkers watched the action. The sports car took off while the kids in the back stuck their fists out the windows and shouted, "Whoo-hoo!"

Meanwhile the film crew on the truck paralleled them, shooting video with the panorama of Arches' red rocks in the background.

Then Mom heard a siren. She glanced in her mirror and noticed flashing lights from a ranger patrol car quickly approaching. Is this part of the action? she wondered.

The patrol car pulled up next to the Parkers and the ranger hurriedly explained something to the flagperson. She got on her radio and relayed the message to the film crew. She listened to their response and then the car and filming immediately stopped.

The ranger patrol car zoomed past the scene with lights flashing.

The flagperson approached the Parkers again. "You can go now too. They're going to have to start all over."

As Mom inched past the film crew, James pondered, "I wonder where that ranger is going in such a hurry."

Mom accelerated to normal speed. Then Morgan leaned forward in the back seat. "Would you buy that car, Mom and Dad? It looks cool."

"It depends on the gas mileage and reliability," Mom replied.

"Looks just aren't enough," Dad added.

"Ohhhh," Morgan laughed. "Sometimes you guys are way too practical."

The family drove on, passing more spectacular sections of Arches' rockbound scenery. As the road continued to climb, they noticed a giant boulder perched on a rock pedestal ahead. "That must be Balanced Rock!" James exclaimed.

Mom pulled over into the parking lot next to it. They gazed from their car at the massive 3,500-ton boulder sitting on top of a rock pinnacle. "I wonder how long that will stay up there," Dad mused.

Morgan, James, Mom, and Dad spent a few minutes wandering around Balanced Rock. As they circled the formation, Morgan took pictures from various angles. Then they piled back into the car and drove on.

Balanced Rock

What Goes Up, Must Come Down

Mom took a side road toward the Windows area. As they approached the end of the short drive, Morgan noticed a huge hole in one of the reddish rocks. Then she saw another. "Look at those giant arches!" she called out excitedly.

"Now we know why this area is called the Windows," Mom said.

Several park ranger vehicles were at the Windows parking area, including the one that had zoomed by the family at the roadblock. "This must be where the emergency is," Dad stated.

The Parkers began walking on the short loop trail, heading toward Turret Arch. In the distance to the east were the giant, circular arches called the North and South Windows.

"Is there any other place in the world like this?" Mom said.

Morgan, James, Mom, and Dad climbed a small hill and came upon a large, vertical hole in the rock. The trail led right toward the massive opening. "Let's go!" Mom said with enthusiasm.

The Parkers scrambled through Turret Arch, looking directly up at it as they passed underneath.

Large boulders were scattered below the arch. "We definitely don't want to stay in here too long," Dad

HOW MANY ARCHES ARE THERE?

There are over two thousand known natural arches in Arches National Park. There are also many more holes in rocks and other unusual as well as spectacular rock formations.

said, noticing the cracks in the rocks of the arch, "in case gravity decides to do its thing."

Right on the other side of the opening, a family was gathered with several rangers. Ropes and other gear were strewn about.

"We're setting up a belay right now," one ranger said into a hand radio. "Yes. He climbed up, but couldn't get down. That's right—just on the other side of Turret Arch—that nemesis spot again."

The Parkers paused to watch the proceedings. A teenage boy and a ranger were near the top of a steep, rocky chute. The ranger had looped a rope around the boy and was giving him instructions.

"Just slide down to the next hold—it's only a few feet below. Don't worry. I've got you, and I'm not going to let you fall."

The boy followed the prompt. He cautiously lowered himself and then glanced down at his nervous family. "Sorry. It was a lot easier going up," he called while placing a foot against a protruding rock.

"It's okay," the boy's mom replied. "We just want you to be back on the ground safely."

"What goes up must come down," one of the rangers remarked. "You're not the first rescue we've had here at infamous Turret Arch."

The ranger continued to guide the teenager slowly back to safety. Finally, as they got close to the bottom, the boy turned to him and said, "I think I can make it the rest of the way."

"Go ahead," the ranger said, keeping him on the rope but letting out a little slack.

A moment later the boy was back on level ground. He slipped out of the rope and explained, "I lost my confidence on those first few steps down." Then he looked toward where he had been stuck near the top of the chute. "If I didn't get spooked, I think I could have made it."

"Better that you came down in one piece," the boy's father said.

Mom turned toward the rest of her family. "I think we should go," she whispered.

Morgan, James, and Dad took Mom's hint and moved on.

"I'm sorry for all the trouble" was the last thing the Parkers heard the boy sheepishly say.

Meanwhile Morgan, James, Mom, and Dad slipped back through Turret Arch and onto the main trail. From that vantage point they could see the North and South Windows in the distance separated by a large bulge of rock. "That looks like someone's nose and glasses," Morgan remarked.

"That's why they call it the Spectacles," Dad responded.

Instead of hiking directly toward the Windows, the Parkers opted for the primitive trail around the back side. They hiked along, enjoying the solitude of their choice while watching people in the distance climbing into one of the windows.

The Spectacles at sunrise

"No one is in this area. We've got it all to ourselves," James remarked.

"Just the way I like it," Dad added.

The trail led the family back to their car. But first they detoured across the parking lot to the short Double Arch Trail.

Soon the Parkers approached two massive, reddish-beige-colored arches spanning a section of rock walls. "They're shaped like rainbows," James noted.

"Or huge elephant trunks," Morgan added.

Several people were already underneath the gigantic arches, so the Parkers also climbed up. Near the top they scrambled to a notch right below the spans with views in both directions. The family sat there enjoying the immense display of geology.

Double Arch

Mom quickly pulled out her sketch pad and began drawing the scenery. Morgan snapped several photos. Dad stared straight up and commented, "Geology is amazing."

After taking a few more photos, Morgan glanced about, noticing all the bizarre rock formations nearby and a slew of boulders strewn beneath Double Arch.

A tiny trickle of rocks rolled down somewhere. Morgan tried to pick out the origin of the small cascade. She looked up at the massive, precariously positioned rock spans and again studied the large boulders below. Then Morgan noticed that Dad and James were also staring at the displaced rocks.

"Are you thinking what I'm thinking?" Dad said to the twins.

"Yes!" they both nodded. "What goes up must come down," Morgan recalled.

Mom threw her sketch pad into her pack. "Let's go then."

And the Parkers trekked back to their car.

Is That You in the Mirror?

Later that day the Parkers exited their car in a large, already-filled parking lot. They packed up water, lathered on sunscreen, and began a one-and-a-half-mile ascent to Utah's most famous landmark. The warm September sunshine streamed down between puffy cumulus clouds.

The family skirted the remains of Wolfe Ranch. Morgan snapped a few photos of the remnant, historic cabin.

Wolfe Ranch cabin

The wide path was filled with a multitude of hikers. "This sure is a popular spot," James observed.

"I think," Dad remarked, "that when we get to the top we'll understand why."

At first the trail rolled up and down. Along the way Dad wiped sweat from his brow. But then the sun vanished behind a cloud, and it suddenly felt a little cooler.

Soon the dirt trail turned into solid rock. All the hikers were heading up, following a worn pathway. "I guess that's the route," Mom said, leading the way.

The family climbed the steady, steep path. They passed a few dry water holes along the way.

Meanwhile, clouds had built up in the sky, and shade occasionally cooled the line of sightseers.

A few sprinkles began falling. Morgan extended her arms to catch as many of the drops as she could. "It's raining!" she announced.

James mimicked his sister with his arms. "And it's cooler out. Yeah!"

Suddenly larger drops began falling, briefly polka-dotting the slickrock surface before almost instantly evaporating.

"It feels so good!" Morgan called out while catching a few raindrops on her palms.

"Hey, there's a little rainbow," James noticed, pointing toward the sky.

Then, as quickly as the shower started, it stopped, and the rock pavement immediately dried up.

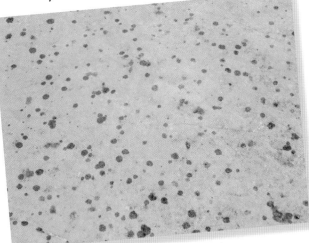

Raindrops on slickrock

Farther along, two people had scrambled into a hole in the rock just above the trail. "Look, an arch!" Mom called out.

Morgan, James, Mom, and Dad briefly watched the pair. They were both holding onto their hats. "The wind is really blasting us up here," one of them called down.

"It looks like they're getting a Moab Facial," Morgan said to her family.

Then one of their hats blew off and tumbled right toward the Parkers. James grabbed it before it could whisk off into the nearby canyon. "Let's get out of here," the hatless hiker called to his companion.

The trail to Delicate Arch

The two people quickly scurried down. They hopped back onto the trail, next to the Parkers. James handed the hat back. "Thanks," the man replied.

"What did you see up there?" Dad asked.

"An arch through an arch," the man replied. "But the second arch is the one we are all looking for, and it's right around the corner."

Morgan, James, Mom, and Dad followed the two people up the trail. Just ahead a large crowd of hikers was gathered at a circular, rock amphitheater. The Parkers picked up their pace in anticipation.

The rock wall paralleling the trail gave way to an open bowl. At the far side of the bowl was a stunningly positioned, gigantic arch perched all by itself. The photogenic natural window framed the distant La Sal Mountains behind it.

THE MAKING OF AN ARCH

The Arches National Park area sits on top of a salt bed that is responsible for the arches, spires, and rock formations in the park. The salt bed was deposited by ancient seas and then covered by mud and water from floods. This mixture eventually cemented into rock. Over time the salt layer buckled and flowed, thrusting some sections upward. This caused parts of the salt layer to dome up and crack. Water seeped into the cracks, eroding away some areas and cementing others, leaving behind freestanding fins of rock. During colder periods, ice got into the cracks, putting pressure on them through expansion. Over many years this pressure caused parts of some fins to break off, forming holes or arches in a few areas, while other fins just collapsed. The process is still going on today.

The Parkers sat on some rocks along with hordes of others who had hiked up for this view at sunset. They all gazed at Delicate Arch in wonder and awe.

"That might be the best of the best as far as arches go," Dad said.

"Did you know that's Utah's state symbol?" Mom asked.

James nodded. "It's on all the cars' license plates," he added.

Mom took out her sketch pad and started drawing. She held the pad firmly, buffering it against the wind.

Meanwhile it had clouded up again. And along with the wind, a few raindrops showered down.

Morgan noticed a bunch of birds darting about in the air. One flew right through Delicate Arch and then flipped over in midair before turning upright, rising up, and whisking away again. "Did you guys see that?" Morgan called out.

"I think they're cliff swallows," Mom replied.

"They're like airborne gymnasts," Dad added.

Suddenly larger splats of rain began falling. Soon the rock surface became completely wet and the wind picked up. "It's actually kind of cool now," Mom said, quickly putting her sketch pad away.

The rain came down harder. Dad examined the sky, noticing dark clouds in some places, but clearing on other parts of the horizon.

The Parkers looked at the arch. "I wonder how long we should stay here," Dad said. "The area is very exposed."

Meanwhile other visitors were scurrying for cover. Then Mom got an idea. "Follow me!" she called out.

The family scrambled back down the trail. Mom found the spot where the two people with the hats had been before. She quickly stepped up onto the rock and gave Morgan and James a hand. Dad followed.

They all scampered into the hole in the rock. "Our little shelter," Mom announced.

Morgan, James, Mom, and Dad scrunched together inside the smaller arch. They gazed out at visitors taking photos of Delicate Arch and then dashing for cover as sheets of rain now pummeled the area.

The Parkers waited out the storm, partially protected from the onslaught. Rain kept pouring down, and suddenly water was cascading everywhere off the rocks.

At one point James leaned forward and inspected the area. "Hey, look!" he called out.

A muddy waterfall was pouring down a rock formation across the way.

"There's another one over there," Morgan exclaimed.

A moment later the rain let up. The sun quickly returned and everything began to dry. The newly created waterfalls quickly came to a stop, and steam began wafting off the rocks.

Dad crawled outside and checked the sky. Then he crept back in to his family. "I think this is our moment of opportunity," he said.

"Wait," Morgan called out. "Let me get a picture first."

Morgan took a photo of her family looking at Delicate Arch through the arch they were in.

"What a place," Dad exclaimed as they scampered back to the main trail.

"But it probably wasn't the best spot to hang out during a storm," Mom admitted. "We were quite vulnerable to lightning." Mom reflected for a second. "Let's put it this way. I wouldn't recommend it to anyone. But in that situation, it might have been our best option."

As Morgan, James, Mom, and Dad trekked back down the trail, the sun continued to shine on the wet rocks. Meanwhile more evening hikers were streaming up to the arch.

"It's like a little pilgrimage to this place," Mom said, noticing all the people.

Soon the Parkers came to the dry potholes they had passed on the way up. But now they were full of water, and small cascades trickled down from one hole to the next.

Mom led the family to one of the brand-new miniature pools. She stood over the clear water and gazed into it. Morgan and James joined her. The three of them stared at their reflections.

James patted his hair down. "I look like I've been camping in the desert for a long time."

"Yeah, I hardly recognize myself," Morgan said, gazing into the mirrored pool.

Mom studied the water closely. "I don't see anything moving yet," she announced.

Dad wandered over. "What would be alive in that now? It was dry until a few minutes ago."

"Lots of things," Mom answered. "And if we hung around, we'd soon see some of the tiny creatures. We'll check some other water holes, if they don't evaporate."

Suddenly the wind picked up again. Fine particles of sand blasted the family's faces.

Mom stood up, feeling her irritated skin. "Now I know what the ranger meant by a 'facial' out here!" she exclaimed.

"We're all getting one," Dad added, covering his face with his arms.

"Soon we'll all have beautiful, youthful-looking skin again," Morgan announced, mocking a commercial.

"Very funny," Mom said sarcastically. Then she led her family quickly down the trail. "I've had enough of this facial for now."

Muscle Man Poses

The next morning the family got up before sunrise. They packed up food and hiking supplies and quietly walked out of the campground.

Across the way, a series of towering rock fins were silhouetted against the early morning sky.

Soon the Parkers arrived at the Devils Garden trailhead. "The coup de grâce of hiking in Arches," Dad exclaimed. "At least that's what I've read."

"Hey, look, a rabbit!" Morgan called out.

The small animal twitched its nose while looking at the Parkers. Then it scampered into the cover of a nearby bush.

The family stopped at the drinking fountain at the trailhead. The large parking lot was almost empty. "The trail is ours for now," Mom boasted.

Morgan, James, Mom, and Dad filled their water bottles and began walking on a wide, gravelly path.

They hiked between two large rock fins and entered Devils Garden. Before sunrise the area was a palette of pinkish-hued rocks against a soft blue sky. The Parkers trudged along, hearing only the sound of their footsteps on the trail.

At the top of a small rise, Dad held out his arms to stop his family. "Look over there," he said quietly, pointing ahead.

Farther up the trail was a scrawny, tan-colored animal. "A coyote," Mom whispered.

The mammal crossed the path well in front of the Parkers. "Hey, Mr. Coyote," Dad called to alert the animal that the family was there.

Devils Garden

The coyote turned and stared at the Parkers. Then something else got its attention. Suddenly it bolted toward the bushes.

A tiny rabbit ran out of the brush and randomly zigzagged ahead of the coyote. The coyote lunged after the small furry creature, but the rabbit dashed into the protection of a bush.

The coyote frantically searched around the plant, sniffing and pawing up sand here and there. Then the coyote jumped onto the bush. The rabbit took off again with the coyote in full pursuit.

In the nick of time the rabbit scampered into a hole in the ground and disappeared.

The coyote circled the area and pawed furiously at the dirt, kicking up more sand and debris. After a while it trotted off.

"Well, that was sure exciting," Dad announced and resumed walking.

"I'm glad nothing gory happened," Mom added.

After taking short spur trails to Pine Tree and Tunnel Arches, the family returned to the main trail. "I'm going to have to write down the names of these arches," Morgan announced, "so I can remember them for my photos."

Suddenly the first rays of morning sun lit up the top of the rock fins. Morgan immediately began snapping more pictures. Soon after, the whole area was bathed in bright sunlight.

Meanwhile the Parkers walked on, approaching a gigantic, thin sliver of rock spanning an expansive stretch of air.

"Wow," Dad gasped. "Landscape Arch. The largest one on earth."

The family walked over to an information sign below the arch. They all studied the sign and the arch. "It's over three hundred feet across," James read.

HOW LONG WILL IT LAST?

Landscape Arch really is defying gravity. But it might not for that much longer. The precarious span is over three hundred feet long but only eleven feet thick at its thinnest point. On September 1, 1991, a seventy-three-foot section of the arch fell out of the narrowest area, reducing its thickness from sixteen to eleven feet. Then, on June 5, 1995, another forty-seven-foot mass of rock fell, followed by another round of gravity-induced collapse of thirty more feet on June 21, 1995. Due to this activity, the short loop trail underneath the arch is now closed. Landscape Arch could collapse at any time.

Landscape Arch, the longest arch on the planet

"And part of it collapsed in 1991," Morgan added.

"Hmm," Dad said when he finished reading the sign. "I guess 'shift happens.' Geology never stops."

Morgan and James glanced at their father, smirking. "For a second I thought you said something else," Morgan said suspiciously.

"Not me!" Dad exclaimed. "I'm innocent!"

The family continued on, climbing between rocky fins and a large pile of rubble. "I wonder what came down around here," Mom commented.

They took another side trail to Partition Arch. Mom took a photo of the twins framed in the window of sandstone.

Navajo Arch

The Parkers then wandered over to Navajo Arch. This thick span of stone had a Christmas tree–shaped juniper growing right underneath the middle of it.

"I can imagine this decorated with lights," Morgan called out enthusiastically.

"And plenty of ornaments," Dad added, touching one of the needles.

Mom laughed and then commented about all the holes in the rocks. "Every one of these arches is so beautiful and so unique."

The family clambered back to the main trail. Now the pathway led right, to the top of one of the rock fins.

The Parkers scampered up. "We're on top of the world!" Dad announced.

As they traversed the rock fin, James noticed his enlarged shadow, paralleling him to the left. He stopped and made a muscular pose. "Hey, look at me!"

Muscle man pose

Morgan, Mom, and Dad watched James. Then they too posed for the benefit of their shadows.

Finally Mom suggested, "Let's all hold our arms up."

The family did, and Morgan took another picture.

Meanwhile the trail continued across the top of the rock fin. The family hiked along, staying toward the middle of the fin to avoid the drop-offs on each side. "This is my favorite part of the trail," Morgan exclaimed while hopping from one part of the rock to another.

Slowly they began to work their way back down. The Parkers stopped briefly at Black Arch overlook, then turned a corner and saw two large, circular holes in a rock wall.

"Double O Arch," Mom called out. "We made it."

They scrambled down to the last named arch on the trail. The family found a shady area to sit in.

"Breakfast time," Dad announced, and he and Mom began unpacking food.

Double O Arch

The Rabbit's Foot

After eating, the Parkers sat in the shade admiring the two circles carved geologically out of the rock.
Morgan got up for a better view. She started climbing a small sand dune, then glanced down at the fine red sand.

"Hey!" Morgan called out. "Look at these!"

James immediately jumped up to join his sister. Together they stared down at the jumbled mass of tracks crisscrossing the sand. "Boy, something sure has been busy around here," James reported.

Mom and Dad also hurried over. The Parkers studied the maze of markings in the sand. "It looks like a convoluted series of miniature freeway junctions," Dad described.

"And from different creatures," Morgan added. "The tracks aren't all the same."

"What do you think they're from?" James asked.

"These look like lizard," Mom said. "We've seen so many of them."

Rabbit tracks

"And this smooth trail. That could be a snake," Dad pointed out. "I know they're out here."

"This one looks like little paws," James called out.

"Rabbit!" all four Parkers said at once.

Morgan followed the rabbit tracks up the mound of sand. She noticed a different pair of tracks near the top. "These look like dog tracks."

Mom came over. "Most likely they're from a coyote," she reported. "Remember the chase we watched earlier?"

Dad surveyed the whole area. "One more reason to come out here early. Not only did we beat the heat, but soon this whole little pile of evidence from last night's action will be trampled by hikers."

Morgan continued along the rabbit track's path. She searched until she reached a small bush. Something furry with red blotches on it caught her attention. Morgan bent down to inspect the object closer. "Oh, no!"

"What is it?" James asked.

"Part of a rabbit," she replied.

The whole family clambered over. A mangled leg and foot was partially covered by sand and the small bush. The part of the leg that was visible was coated in dried blood.

"Poor thing," Morgan said sadly. "I wonder where the rest of it is."

Mom scanned the area for any predators. "I don't think we want to know all the details."

James also looked around. "Seeing the dead rabbit makes me nervous, but these tracks also gave me some ideas."

James scrambled back to his pack and pulled out his story. "My next chapter starts right now. Okay?"

"Okay," Mom replied. "That'll give me a chance to sketch these two arches."

Meanwhile Morgan and Dad looked at the park map. "Hey," Morgan said, noticing a nearby spur trail to Dark Angel. "Do you want to head over there, Dad?"

"Sure," Dad replied. He looked at James and Mom. "Do you two want to come?"

"I want to write now while my thoughts are fresh," James answered. "Can Mom and I wait here?"

"The trail comes right back to this spot," Morgan said.

"Perfect," Dad added. "We'll be back in about thirty minutes."

James began to write . . .

"Sir. There are large tracks heading up this wash," the young crew member, Parker, reported to Major John Wesley Powell.

James paused from his writing, wondering whether all his characters had been introduced to each other by now. Oh well, I can always change that later if I need to, he concluded. Then James smiled, realizing that he had just added himself to his story.

Major Powell inspected the tracks. "Deer," he said. "Well, it might be worth a try. The crew could use some meat."

"Shall I head up there?"

"Yes. But this time I'll go with you."

Major Powell informed the crew of their plans. "We'll be back in time for supper. After all the food we've lost, I want to take advantage of every opportunity to try and find some game," he explained. Then Powell pointed. "But search for us up there in case we don't return on time."

"That'll give us some time to repair the boats," a crew member said to Powell.

Parker and Powell began trekking up the sandy wash. They followed the tracks until the dry riverbed boxed out at a series of rocks. Powell looked around. "Let's climb up," he suggested.

Parker scaled the slickrock first, checking to see that his rifle was secure while he climbed. At the top of a rise, he turned to watch Powell scramble up the rocky slope using his one arm for balance. "You are amazing," Parker said to Powell.

Major Powell walked on. "Come on. There's a hungry, hopeful crew waiting for us below."

The two continued up the sandstone escarpment. They turned a bend in their makeshift path and stopped. A jagged, triangle-shaped arch spanned a fin of rocks directly in front of them.

"Whoa!" Powell exclaimed. "I surely didn't expect to see anything like this up here."

Parker gulped in astonishment at the giant hole in the rock. He wiped some sweat off his brow and then stared through the large opening, noticing a glare on the other side. "Boy, the heat sure radiates off these rocks," he said, reaching for his canteen. "It's like the Devil himself lives out here."

"Yeah," Powell added. "But to me it's all one big, beautiful rock garden."

Suddenly a cracking sound split the air.

Powell and his companion froze, searching for the source of the unusual noise.

The cracking noise sounded again, only this time louder—like a deafening rumble. The two explorers instinctively looked up. A large chunk of rock was peeling off the arch.

"Look out!" Powell yelled.

The two men bolted from the partially collapsing arch and ducked down, covering their heads with their arms. For several seconds rocks crashed and boomed to the ground, then, gradually, all became quiet.

Powell and Parker lifted their heads up from the ground. A cloud of dust filled the air. The two slowly stood up and brushed themselves off. "Are you okay?" Powell asked.

Parker nodded, then coughed up some dust.

A moment later the dust began to settle and the air cleared. When the two looked up at the arch, it was much smaller and had a pile of rubble beneath . . .

James paused from his writing and looked up. "Hey, Morgan and Dad. You're back!"

Dad glanced at James's notebook. "I see you've been busy. Do we get to hear more soon?"

"Soon," James promised. "When I'm finished. How was Dark Angel?"

"Pretty cool," Morgan replied. "A giant pillar of rock standing all by itself."

Another group of hikers arrived at Double O Arch just as the Parkers packed up. "Desert solitaire no more," Mom mentioned, referring to the book Dad was reading about the region.

Morgan showed the map to her family. "I bet the primitive trail back will be quieter," she suggested.

"Good idea," Mom said. "And it will be new to us, a loop trail."

"And we'll get to see more arches," James added.

And with that, the Parkers headed back.

Dark Angel

Hide and Seek

The Parkers returned to their campsite and then took a quick walk on the surprisingly remote and beautiful Broken Arch Trail.

Once back at camp, Dad lounged in a foldout chair and pulled out his Edward Abbey book. "Time to do nothing!" he announced to the world while stretching out his legs. He opened the book and started reading.

As the late afternoon warmth slowly melted into evening, Morgan noticed people clambering among the rocks throughout the campground.

She grabbed her journal and said to her parents. "I'm going to climb up there. Okay?"

"Okay," Mom replied. "But only to a safe spot that you can also climb down."

Morgan scrambled up a nearby slanted, reddish boulder, pulled out her journal, and wrote:

Dear Diary:

I'm perched above our campsite. But don't worry, the rock I'm on isn't that steep and I won't get stuck up here. But what a great view I have. I can see pillars of stone fins everywhere. And as it gets close to sunset, the rocks seem to light up in color, almost as if they're on fire. No wonder they call part of this place the Fiery Furnace. We'll find out more about that tomorrow.

I can't help but take pictures here. Good thing I have a digital camera—I've taken so many.

What I can't see from where I am, though, are more arches. We did see two new ones on the Broken Arch Trail. Tapestry and Broken Arch are just as neat as any of the others we've been to in the park. And we got to walk right through Broken Arch.

We've also seen several rabbits. There's even one hopping around near our campsite right now. Hopefully the coyotes will stay away from it—and us.

Even though I'm perched on my own private spot on the rocks, I'm not the only one with this idea. There are people climbing all over the place around camp. I just hope no one goes up somewhere where they can't get down.

Guess what? We're camped next to twins! They're two boys. I think they're around six or seven years old. They must be identical because they look so much alike. I don't know how their parents tell them apart. Right now they're chasing each other around the campground. Funny!

More soon from Arches,

Morgan

Morgan put her journal away and watched the twins. Now they seemed to be playing hide and seek. While one closed his eyes and started counting to twenty, the other took off running. He stopped near the Parkers' campsite and crouched behind a rock.

James saw the boy's legs sticking out. "Back here," James whispered, directing him to a better hideout, a narrow slot between large boulders.

Then James came over and helped the younger boy crouch down just as they heard the brother yell, "Twenty!"

The other twin started searching for his brother. Meanwhile James and the boy stayed low, hiding behind the rock. All the while Morgan watched the goings-on from above.

The searching boy called out. "Tommy! Tommy! Where are you?" He continued poking his head here and there but couldn't find him.

Morgan waved at the boy. "Try over there," she hinted, pointing.

The twin headed in the direction of Morgan's prompt. But he ended up right next to the Parkers' tent.

Morgan slid down from her perch and came over to the boy. "This way," she motioned.

Morgan guided the boy to behind the Parkers' campsite. There he saw James and Tommy's legs still sticking out from the rock.

The boy raced over to the rock. "I found you!" he announced.

Morgan also walked up. Then James and Tommy stood up and dusted off their clothes.

Suddenly Morgan gasped. "Don't move!" she said urgently.

One of the twins also saw the danger. "A snake!" he screamed.

Mom and Dad heard the call. So did the other twins' parents. Instantly all four adults were by their kids' sides. Dad inched closer and hoisted James away from the coiled-up reptile. The other mom quickly ushered her two boys away from the snake.

The two families stood at a distance and watched the pinkish snake flick its tongue in and out. Then they noticed the end of its tail.

"A rattlesnake," James murmured.

The exposed snake sensed the intruders. It began to slowly slide sideways toward the rocks. The families backed up a few more feet.

"If we leave it alone," Dad said, "it will leave us alone."

Eventually the snake found protection among some rocks surrounded by bushes. It hid as well as it could there.

"Well, that was interesting," the other father said.

The two families introduced themselves. "We're from San Luis Obispo, California," James said.

"Wow. We're from Santa Cruz," the other mom shared.

"Small world, isn't it?" Dad responded.

Later, at dinner, James kept glancing back at the miniature chasm he and Tommy had been hiding in. "I keep thinking that rattler's going to come out of there," he explained to his family.

But it never did.

Triple Twins

The next afternoon the Parkers joined a group of people at the Fiery Furnace parking lot. A ranger came over and introduced herself. "Welcome, everyone, to trail-less exploring," she announced. "My name is Mariah, and I'm going to take you to my favorite place in the park."

Mariah began leading the crowd down a rocky slope. After entering a ravine, she stopped and gathered everyone together.

"The colored rock layers," Mariah began, pointing at the massive red sandstone slabs, "were formed by many sea episodes of salt deposits and eons of debris accumulation, until the resulting rock got about five thousand feet thick. Erosion from wind and water then stripped away thousands of feet of rock, creating narrow sandstone walls called rock fins. Most of the park's arches are formed from these highly erodible fins."

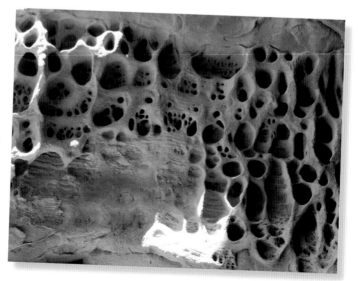

Mariah turned to look forward. "From here on we'll mostly be in washes or on the rocks. We keep the area trail-less so visitors can have a more wild experience, and to help keep the plants, animals, and soil from being disturbed."

"The soil?" someone asked.

"Yep. Please don't disturb the soil by walking on it. I'll explain in a little bit," Mariah said. "Follow me."

As the ranger led the group between a maze of towering rock fins, the Parkers shuffled along with everyone else.

James noticed another family near the front of the group. Two boys were with their parents. "Hey, it's Tommy and his brother!" James announced.

"The twins," Morgan confirmed.

Morgan waved to the boys and they waved back.

Meanwhile Mariah gathered the group together again near a sloping hillside of sand, dirt, and plants.

"See that black layer on the soil?" Mariah pointed to a spot on the ground.

The group looked over.

"Well, it's actually alive. The dark crust is filled with living organisms that help bind the soil together. It also allows plants like these oak and juniper to take hold. It if weren't for that soil, we'd really be getting sandstorms around here.

"So, as we like to say," Mariah quipped, "don't bust the crust. Stay in the washes where it is sandy, or walk only on rocks."

Twins in the Fiery Furnace

The group followed the ranger farther into Fiery Furnace. Soon they approached a dark, shady side canyon. Mariah led everyone directly under a small natural arch and into a sandy area. She smiled and then informed everyone, "You just walked under a bridge."

"Not an arch?" someone asked.

"Nope. But there is an arch in here."

The group looked around.

"Over there!" Tommy pointed above to another hole in the rocks.

"Good eye," Mariah said. "But technically that pothole up there and

the bridge you walked under are not arches."

Then Mariah pointed off to one side. "But look over there."

Up a rocky slope was a small, jagged hole near the bottom of a large rock. "That's an arch!" Mariah stated.

Then she explained. "There are over two thousand arches in this park and

thousands more holes in the rocks. So the park came up with an exact definition of what actually makes an arch. For one thing, it must be at least three feet across. That pothole up there is only two and a half feet."

"What about that bridge?" Dad asked.

"It is more than three feet," Mariah admitted. "But it was created by water running underneath and carving it rather than rocks falling out from it. So we call it Walk Through Bridge. And the one over there is Crawl Through Arch."

"So, does anyone want to crawl through it?"

All the kids in the group raised their hands and started scrambling up toward the small arch.

"Wait a second!" Mariah called out. "I have to go around to the other side first and guide you back down."

Once Mariah was set, one by one the kids slithered through the constricted passage. Morgan and James waved to their parents just before they disappeared to the other side.

When the line of youngsters was through, Dad announced, "Well, I'm still a kid!" And he, along with a few other willing adults, also crawled through the narrow arch.

Then Mariah led everyone back through Walk Through Bridge, and the group continued on. As they hiked, she mentioned, "We've got some larger arches up ahead."

Soon they were in another section of the labyrinth. Again everyone gathered around the ranger. "Has anyone seen any cool things in the park?"

"We saw a snake yesterday!" Tommy exclaimed.

Mariah looked at the two blonde-haired boys. "Hey, you two are twins!" she realized.

The two boys smiled.

Then Mariah asked, "What did the snake look like?"

"It was a rattlesnake," the other twin answered. "It was kind of pink."

"Yes. The faded midget rattlesnake," Mariah explained. "Although they are venomous, they're typically fairly timid. Where did you see it?"

"Near our campsite."

"Just be careful when you're exploring around the rocks," Mariah

Twin Arch

warned. Then she spoke to the group. "Well—it's quite a coincidence that we have twin boys in our group and we're standing under Twin Arch."

Mariah gazed high above. Two large, similarly shaped holes hovered far up the rock wall. "Pretty neat, huh?"

Then Tommy said, "But there're more twins than us here." He looked toward Morgan and James, who stepped up.

Mariah inspected the pair of Parker kids. "You two, also?"

"Yep," Morgan replied. "We're fraternal."

Mariah chuckled. "Now this is definitely a first. Triple sets of twins in this room." Then she gazed at Twin Arches again. "Do you think they're identical or fraternal?"

The group laughed. Then Mariah said, "There's something else in this room I want to show you. Follow me."

Everyone walked over to a shaded area. A small pool of water filled a depression in one of the rocks. "Look in there," Mariah directed.

Morgan bent down for an inspection. "There're bones!" she called out. "That's right," Mariah replied. "What do you think they're from?" Everyone studied what they could see of the leftover animal. There was a skull and foot among the skeletal debris. "A rabbit?" Morgan asked.

"Yep," Mariah replied. "For whatever reason, the ravens bring them here and scatter the remains in this area. This part of Fiery Furnace is sort of a rabbit burial ground. And there's a raven's nest up toward

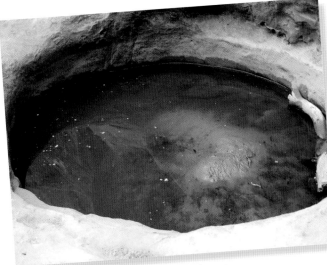

Twin Arches. So maybe that's why they eat nearby." Mariah pointed toward some branches and an area of stained rock perched high above.

"So," Mom turned toward her family. "Maybe it wasn't a coyote that got that rabbit at Double O Arch." Then Mom told the ranger what they had seen on the trail yesterday.

Pothole with bones

"It could have been a coyote," Mariah concluded. "Or a raven. Or both."

The tour continued with Mariah leading the way among a series of rock climbs and scrambles. The group maneuvered past several sections of a maze of slot canyons. Soon they were in an entirely different part of the Fiery Furnace.

"Look over here," Mariah said, pointing to an unusually shaped arch. "We call that one Kissing Turtle."

"I can see the turtle shapes!" James exclaimed.

"Who gets to name these arches?" Mom asked.

"Usually the people who discover them," Mariah replied.

James thought for a second, then stopped walking.

Dad saw the expression on James's face. "What are you thinking about?"

"I'm thinking I left something out of my story."

"What's that?"

"I had John Wesley Powell discover an arch. But he didn't name it."

"Okay," Dad replied. "But that's the beauty of a first draft. You can always change things later. What do you think you'll call it?"

"I don't know yet," James said. "But I have a few ideas because of the shape of the rock I set the arch in."

Mariah led everyone farther. Eventually the group approached a narrow passage. Mariah went first, squeezing through the constricted area between the rocks and then positioning herself at the end. One by one she guided the group through. As James came up to the ranger, he straddled the narrow section with one foot against each rock wall. But his placement wasn't secure, and suddenly James slid into a tighter spot, skinning his knee along the way. "Ow!" James hollered, before quickly bracing himself from falling farther.

Tight passage!

Mariah glanced at James's leg. "Are you okay?" she asked.

James nodded, and with Mariah's help he scampered beyond the narrow passage. James joined Mom and Morgan, and together they watched Dad saunter through.

When Dad came up, he looked at James's knee. "It looks like you got a little rock rash," he assessed. "But no bleeding, that's good. Are you okay to go on?"

James nodded again.

Finally they climbed into another, darker side canyon.

"Come on up and rest for a few minutes," Mariah invited as everyone walked up. "It's nice and shady in here."

Everyone sat down, and then Mariah started another story.

"In 1963 the park superintendent came up here and explored this very room. He had a wide, flat hat on, and he walked right past where all of you are sitting. Farther up, the canyon boxed out and he had to turn around. When he came back here, he heard a bird and looked up."

Mariah paused. "So . . . look up, everyone!"

Spanning the air directly above the group was a beautifully shaped arch in the stone. "Surprise!" Mariah exclaimed.

"Whoa!" several people in the group exclaimed. A few quickly grabbed their cameras and took pictures.

"And so our superintendent named this arch Surprise."

"Surprise Arch?" someone asked for clarification.

"Yep."

Mariah spoke in a whisper. "You know, when Edward Abbey lived here in the 1950s, Arches was a very quiet place. But now we have over 800,000 visitors a year. So, to wrap up our walk, I like having a moment of silence."

Surprise Arch

The group sat still and quiet. Some closed their eyes. Others—like Morgan and James—stared at the arch above them.

After a few minutes Mariah pulled out the book *Desert Solitaire* by Edward Abbey. Morgan recognized the cover. "That's what you're reading, Dad."

"I'd like to share a little bit of this with you," Mariah said while holding up the book.

She cleared her throat. Right then a cracking sound came from somewhere far off. The ranger looked toward the noise and waited a moment.

When it was quiet again, Mariah looked down at her book. Then the group heard a thump in the distance.

"Whoa!" Mariah exclaimed. "So much for our moment of silence."

The ranger quickly scanned the area, including Surprise Arch above them. "Come on," she urged everyone. "It sounds like we're having some geology in action somewhere in the Furnace. And I don't think this is any time to hang out below an arch."

The group scrambled away from the Surprise Arch area. As they trekked along, Mariah pointed to a small boulder twenty feet off the trail. "I bet that's our culprit!" she exclaimed. "That rock wasn't there yesterday. It must have fallen off that fin behind it."

"That could have killed someone," a person in the group said.

Meanwhile, as everyone hurried along, James reflected back to his story. I wrote about something like this happening, he realized.

Finally the group approached a keyhole formation in a notch between rock fins. Across the way were views of the Salt Valley and the Windows area beyond. The tiny pedestal of Balanced Rock appeared in the distance.

Morgan took a picture of her family framed by the keyhole. Then everyone followed Mariah back into the sun and out of Fiery Furnace.

Good-Bye Mom and Dad

Once the Parkers finished the hiking tour, the family reluctantly left the Fiery Furnace area and headed out of the park.

"I'm certainly going to miss this place," Mom commented.

They passed the turnoff to Delicate Arch and then climbed out of the Salt Valley. Next was the junction to the Windows. Shortly after, they passed Balanced Rock, still perched on its pedestal, defying gravity.

After a while the road reached the Courthouse Towers, and the Three Gossips came into view to the west.

"This was where that car commercial was," Morgan recalled.

"Doesn't that seem like such a long time ago?" Mom mused. "We've seen so many interesting things since then."

Finally Dad pulled over at the Park Avenue trailhead. The Parkers piled out of the car and walked over to the viewpoint. They gazed at the towering, thin slabs of rock lining the canyon. The soft blue early evening sky provided a stark contrast to the shadowed, darkened, reddish rock walls.

"It makes me want to sketch some more," Mom said, gesturing toward the view.

"It makes me want to sit and soak in the scenery," Dad added.

James pulled out his map and Morgan came over to look. Then Morgan gazed into the canyon and saw a few people walking along a faint path. "Yep. There's a trail down there."

Suddenly Morgan got an idea. She excitedly shared it with James. Then they both turned to their parents.

"Can we hike down there?" Morgan asked. "It's only a mile."

"But then we'd have to come back up," Dad responded, feeling a little tired from the long day.

Park Avenue

Mom glanced up from her drawing. "I'd really like to sketch for a little bit," she said. "You don't see views like this very often, especially with this evening sky."

Dad stared down into the canyon. He watched the groups of hikers weaving their way along the trail. Then he turned to James. "Can I see the map for a minute?"

Dad looked over the area on the map. Park Avenue Trail was noted to the side as "moderately easy" and only a mile. And if taken one-way, it came out at the Courthouse Towers.

"Hmm," Dad pondered. Then he focused on Morgan and James. "You really want to hike?"

"Yes!" they both replied while nodding their heads enthusiastically.

Dad glanced toward Mom. He walked over to her and discussed his thoughts. After a couple of minutes, they both approached the twins.

Dad took a deep breath and announced, "We think that the two of you certainly have shown you have the experience and wherewithal to hike in the desert. Would you like to do the walk on your own?"

"Can we?" Morgan asked, with an excited but disbelieving expression on her face.

"Yep," Mom chimed in. "Dad and I can hang out here for a bit, then skedaddle back to the Courthouse Towers and pick you up."

"Yes!" James exclaimed. And he and Morgan high-fived.

Dad dashed to the car and grabbed a fanny pack along with snacks and water. "Here's some survival gear," he said when he returned.

"How much time do you think you'll need?" Mom asked.

Morgan shrugged. "I don't know. Maybe half an hour?"

"That sounds about right," Mom replied. "But take your time and enjoy your adventure. We know it will be a beautiful hike."

Morgan and James hugged their parents. Then they proceeded down the rock stairs and into the canyon. Once at the bottom they turned around and waved.

"Good-bye, Mom and Dad!" James called out.

Mom and Dad waved back. Then Dad put his arm around Mom. "Our babies are growing up," he said.

Morgan looked at James as they hiked. "This is so cool!" she exclaimed.

Mom and Dad stood at the trailhead, watching their children wander farther down the canyon. Then Mom resumed sketching. Dad gazed at the towering, thin formations lining Park Avenue like rock skyscrapers.

A short while later James turned to look for his parents again. He could still see them—Dad was using his binoculars and Mom appeared to be drawing. "I'm going to try and not look at them anymore," James announced. "I don't want them to think we're nervous."

"Good idea," Morgan agreed.

An evening breeze cooled the air. Dad glanced down, looking for the twins. "They're out of sight now," he reported.

Mom closed her sketch pad. "Shall we go get them then?"

"Okay."

• • •

James and Morgan continued following the rock cairns and footprints, now in a sandy wash. Something scurried in the bushes. Morgan glanced over and saw a lizard scamper for cover. She and James continued along.

A moment later James abruptly stopped. "Look, a rabbit!"

But Morgan was busy studying some tiny eroded formations and carved pockets along a rock wall. "These are so bizarre!" she exclaimed. "They look like little shelves for trinkets and jewelry." One of the mini shelves had a tiny pile of rocks in it. "Look at what someone put in here, James," she said, pointing to the spot.

Morgan and James hiked on as the sun disappeared behind some towering rock walls. The sound of their footsteps crunched as they walked.

They turned a corner. "There's the parking lot," James called out.

"And our car," Morgan added.

Mom and Dad heard voices coming from the canyon. They glanced in the direction of the trail. "Let's look away and pretend we're busy," Mom said. She gazed over toward the Three Gossips while Dad stared at a small arch in the distance. But out of the corner of his eye he saw two heads bobbing up and down as they approached from the canyon.

Soon Morgan and James reached the highway. They checked both ways then bounded across the road to the parking lot with their supposedly preoccupied parents.

"Hi!" Morgan called out.

Mom acted surprised and looked over. "Hi!" she called back. "That sure was quick."

"Well. How was it?" Dad inquired, smiling.

Morgan and James both reported the details.

"We saw a rabbit."

"And a bunch of lizards."

"And our voices echoed."

"The trail was actually pretty easy."

"We lost the tracks a few times in the wash but then found them again."

"The views of the rocks were amazing."

"You would have liked it."

"I regretted not going as soon as you left," Dad admitted. "But I didn't want to bother you."

"You could have caught up to us," James said. "That would have been great!"

"Well, there's always next time," Mom said.

"And there will definitely be a next time," Dad added. "Come on, you two, let's head into town."

The family returned to their car and left Arches National Park behind for a night at a hotel in Moab.

Cowboys and Indians

The night in town with fresh food, warm showers, and laundry rejuvenated the Parkers for their next adventure. In the morning they drove down US Highway 191, eventually turning west on Highway 211 toward the Needles district in Canyonlands National Park.

The road wound deeper into more remote and rocky areas. The family stared at the mesmerizing scenery surrounding them. "The Needles, here we come," Dad announced.

Eventually Mom pulled the car over at Newspaper Rock, and the Parkers piled out. They wandered over to a vertical slab of rock protected by a fence.

"Wow, look at this," Dad said as he examined the multitude of etchings embedded on the rock wall.

James noticed the human and animal figures. "I wonder what it all means."

Morgan walked up to the sign by the fence and quickly skimmed the words. "It says here that no one is actually sure."

"I certainly can see how the rock got its name," Mom added. "There must be so many stories written in this stone."

Then Dad glanced at James. "Hey, have you written any more sections of your story?"

Petroglyphs on Newspaper Rock

"I'm waiting for the Needles and the river," James replied. "But this sure gets me thinking."

Morgan snapped a few photos of the ancient rock art and then the family climbed back into the car and drove on.

Soon the remote, wild canyons of the Needles district came into view. The Parkers reentered Canyonlands National Park and stopped at the visitor center to get their permits for their backpacking trip to Chesler Park.

"Have a good time out there," the ranger stated. "I think it's one of the best places in the world."

The family filled up their water bottles and walked back to the car. They stopped at a few short trails on their way to the campground. The Roadside Ruin Trail led them to a small granary tucked under a cliff, similar to what they had seen their first day in the park.

Then the family took the short gravel road to Cave Spring. There they took a walk to one of Canyonlands' only permanent sources of water outside of the river.

Mom looked around at all the plants at the start of the trail. "It's so green here compared to most of the park," she commented.

Soon the path led to a large alcove of overhanging rock. Underneath were the remains of a camp.

The Parkers stood behind a fence and inspected the artifacts from a distance.

"It looks like a scene from an old Western movie," Dad said.

"Yeah, a cowboy outpost site," Mom added. "And I don't think it was that long ago that they were out here."

CAVE SPRING

In the late 1800s cowboys settled in the canyons that now make up the area around Canyonlands National Park. John Albert Scorup was one of the best-known cowboys, and he ran a large cattle operation there. Scorup and his partners at one point had up to ten thousand cattle in the area. The ranchers that helped had to stay out on the range with their cattle as they wandered the vast lands of the ranch. They had several camps; one was near Cave Spring. This particular outpost was established at this location because the spring provided a reliable source of water. In 1975 cattle ranching ended within the national park, but many of the artifacts such as the ones at Cave Spring remain.

Cave Spring

The trail continued meandering along under the alcoves. "I love being in the shade," James mentioned.

Soon the Parkers entered a second cave. "Look. Water," Morgan pointed.

The trickle of water flowing out of the cave led to a mossy seep at the back. Mom walked over, noticing a few tiny ferns growing near the source of the water. "Pretty unusual to see these in the desert, don't you think?" she said, touching one of the small green plants. There was no reply.

Mom turned to see what her family was doing. Morgan was staring trans-fixed at the ceiling of the alcove. Dad and James noticed her gaze and joined her. Mom looked at what appeared to be three hypnotized family members. "What do you all see?" she asked.

"Come here," Dad whispered.

All four Parkers stared at the cave's ceiling. On it were several rust-colored handprints and an ancient image of a face.

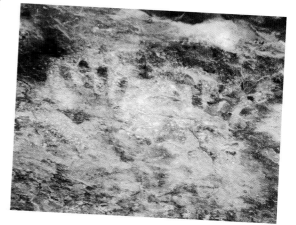
Handprints

"It's kind of spooky," Mom remarked.

"And pretty cool," James added.

The Parkers studied the ancient art for a few more minutes and then trekked on. Soon the trail reached a ladder leading straight up the rock. Morgan and James scaled it first, then Mom and Dad carefully climbed the steep steps. A second ladder led to the top of the rocks.

When they all were gathered on top, Mom looked around and announced, "It's like a whole new trail up here!"

The Parkers followed rock cairns across the slickrock. Eventually the trail looped back toward where it started, and the Parkers returned to their car.

Later the Parkers followed the short Pothole Point Trail to a bunch of potholes in the desert slickrock.

Cairns on the Cave Spring Trail

Potholes, or depressions in the desert sandstone, are often briefly filled with water by intermittent rains. But at other times temperatures can exceed 140 degrees F on the ground, and these empty pockets that once held water seem lifeless. However, lying dormant in the sand are hundreds of microscopic creatures and eggs that have adapted to the extreme conditions. Some of the creatures waiting to spring to life include snails, crustaceans, tadpoles, worms, fairy shrimp, mosquito larvae, beetles, and gnat larvae. Some of these creatures go through what is called cryptobiosis, a process where they lose almost all their body water. Then when it rains, they can rehydrate and come to life within thirty minutes! Potholes are also temporary watering holes for birds, mammals, and reptiles. Because the water is so precious to these life forms, people should not disturb it. That includes keeping hands and feet out— even the oil from our skin can pollute the water, making these rare desert oases uninhabitable for the creatures that live in them.

POTHOLES

James gazed into a dry, dusty pothole. The family recalled what Mom had mentioned on the Delicate Arch Trail. "It's hard to imagine all the eggs, tadpoles, snails, and things that are in there waiting to come to life," James said.

"But they are," Morgan reminded her brother. "So we shouldn't step in it."Finally the family took one more hike, the Slickrock Foot Trail, before settling in to Squaw Flat Campground for the evening.

The spacious campground had sites nestled against large rocks. The Parkers picked a spot and ate dinner while staring out at the rock-strewn horizon.

Meanwhile the sun slowly sank in the sky, lighting up the rocks with a pinkish, fiery hue. Mom got up to begin clearing the table before dark. As she walked back to the car, she noticed animal tracks in the sand. "I wonder," she mused. "Were these from a dog, or a mountain lion, or a coyote?"

The rest of the family came over. The large tracks were partially covered by shoe prints. "It's too hard to tell," Dad remarked. Then Mom shuffled her feet over the tracks. "Best to not worry about it," she concluded.

Please Don't Hurt My Baby

Early the next morning the Parkers ate breakfast and tore down their camp. They loaded up the car and drove on a nearby dirt road to the Elephant Hill parking area.

As the car bounced along, Dad glanced at the rock-strewn world outside. "I feel like we're in the outback somewhere," he commented.

Mom reflected back for a moment. "The scenery here is reminding me of that John Wesley Powell quote you read us in your story, James."

"You mean . . ." James recalled. "The landscape everywhere away from the river is rock, cliffs of rock, tables of rock, plateaus of rock, terraces of rock, crags of rock . . ."

"That's the one!" Mom exclaimed.

"It is amazing country," Dad agreed.

Soon the family arrived at the remote parking lot. They loaded their packs with food, gear, and water. Then Dad placed a sunshade inside the car's window. "Hopefully it won't be an oven in here when we get back."

"Here we go then," Mom announced, leading the way to the trailhead.

The path immediately climbed up a series of rock stairs. Soon the Parkers were high above the parking area.

Morgan took a glance back. "Good-bye, car," she called out.

"And air conditioning," James added.

"Well, at least it's September," Dad replied. "Can you imagine being out here in July?"

The trail leveled out for a time. Before long the Parkers got their first glimpse of the towering, colorful, needled spires of rock looming ahead.

"Wow!" Dad exclaimed. "Look at what's up there."

Soon the family passed by a giant mushroom-shaped rock. A group of hikers were hanging out in the shade underneath it. The two groups waved to each other as Morgan, James, Mom, and Dad tramped by.

CANYONLANDS' MUSHROOM-SHAPED ROCKS

The Needles area is famous for red and white pinnacles of sandstone. The white layer is from beach sand material from the many sea episodes in the area. This rock is naturally cemented together with calcium carbonate, which makes it highly erosion resistant. The red layer is from sedimentary rock, which is much more erodible. When water came through the area, many of these pinnacles were carved away along the weaker red layers, leaving behind caps of white sandstone and creating the mushroom shapes seen today.

The twins noticed the dark, crusty, bacteria-laden dirt everywhere around the trail. "Crypto . . . biotic soil!" Morgan recalled, taking a second to remember the pronunciation.

"And lizards," James added, as one scampered toward the bushes and right over the blackened dirt crust.

Cryptobiotic soil

The Parkers soon fell into a rhythm, walking among the silent stone-laden scenery. The trail at times meandered across flatter, grassy areas with brief interludes of shade between rocks.

Soon they reached a junction. James pulled out his map of the Chesler Park area. "Okay, one and a half miles gone," he announced.

Mom paused to admire the views. "Let's have some water here," she said.

After drinking, the Parkers continued on their journey with Dad now leading the way.

After a while the family came upon a large, shady crack between the rocks. The Parkers stopped for a few minutes, enjoying the interlude out of the sun.

Mom took a deep breath, inhaling the air. "It's so much cooler in here," she mentioned.

Meanwhile James pulled out the map again, studying the trail they were on. Then he glanced at other sections of the map. The names of nearby park features jumped out at him. James cleared his throat and began announcing: "Harvest Scene, Needles, The Fins, Castle Arch."

"Go on." Dad said. "I want to hear what else is out here."

"Let's see," James searched some more. "Lizard Rock. The Doll House. The Plug. Wedding Ring Arch. Caterpillar Arch. Devils Kitchen."

"There're lots of interesting places to explore, that's for sure," Mom said while hoisting her pack back on.

The family left the cool, shady oasis and tramped on. They followed rock piles up and down the uneven terrain. Soon they reached their second trail junction.

Morgan read the sign. "That's 2.1 miles gone," she announced.

"It's less than a mile to Chesler Park," James realized.

Dad scanned the area. "It's good that these signs are out here," he acknowledged. "Without them, this convoluted rock wilderness could easily make us feel lost."

After a few more climbs and descents, the family approached the seemingly impenetrable needled barrier framing Chesler Park.

Another junction indicated only 0.2 mile left to their destination. Morgan, James, Mom, and Dad scrambled up the last section. At the top of the rise, they finally gazed into the Chesler Park arena, a circle-shaped grassland surrounded by towering rock spires and pinnacles. Not another person was in sight.

Trail sign in Chesler Park

"I couldn't even imagine a place so beautiful," Dad whispered in awe.

"And it's so different than a typical mountain backpack," Mom added.

After Morgan snapped a few photos, James checked the map again. "It's this way." He pointed to the left, beyond a junction.

And so the Parkers began hiking toward their backcountry campsite. The trail rolled over small, sandy hills, making the going slow. A few

wildflowers and pincushion cactuses decorated the ground right next to the path.

Suddenly Mom stopped. "Look at these," she called out with alarm. Two large sets of tracks crisscrossed the sandy trail.

"One looks doglike but more pointed, so it's probably a coyote," Mom explained.

"And these?" Dad asked, standing near the other tracks.

Mom inspected them too. "Those," Mom slowly said, "are catlike. Notice the five sections and no claw markings. Cats retract their claws when walking. A large cat out here means a mountain lion."

Morgan and James inched closer to their parents.

Dad scanned the Chesler Park area. "We need to stay close together and definitely keep our eyes open."

The Parkers hiked on. A few minutes later Mom stopped at a small pile of fur-coated scat next to the trail. "Oh, yes. We definitely aren't the only mammals out here!" she remarked.

Still later Mom held out her arms and stopped again. Then she turned to her family and whispered, "Shhh."

The Parkers stood on the sandy trail and watched a small grayish bird hop along about twenty feet ahead of them on the path.

Mom inched closer to get a better look.

The bird wobbled then hopped forward before making a faint call that sounded distressed.

Again Mom took a small step toward the tiny bird. She watched it scoot farther along the path and chirp loudly. "It looks hurt," she guessed.

The bird continued to hop short distances up the trail. The Parkers meanwhile inched forward along the same path, keeping a set distance from the injured bird.

"I'm not sure it can fly," Dad said.

"Or where it is hurt," Mom added.

The gray bird continued scooting along, several yards ahead of the Parkers.

"It's staying on our trail," Morgan whispered.

Suddenly, a larger, distinctly blue bird dropped off the limbs of a nearby juniper tree and flew directly at the Parkers. The bird gathered speed and aimed right at Dad's head.

Dad saw the bluebird at the last second. "Ahhh!" he yelled while ducking.

The bluebird whisked away and flew back to the tree.

"Wow!" Dad exclaimed. "That bluebird just dive-bombed me!"

"Here it comes again," James called out.

The bluebird again flew right at the Parkers. This time it beelined straight for Mom, and as she ducked, the bird whisked off and retreated to its tree.

"Whoa!" Mom called out. "Now that was close."

"That bird on the trail must be its baby," Morgan realized.

"I was thinking that," Mom said. "But I wasn't sure because of the different color."

The bluebird in the tree squawked. The baby bird on the trail chirped back, still meekly hopping along.

Then the bluebird dove at the Parkers again, this time narrowly missing Morgan's ear as it peeled off at the last second.

The Parkers huddled together. "What do we do?" James called out.

"Duck!" Morgan screamed as again they were attacked.

Female mountain bluebird

The bluebird in the tree repeatedly dove at the family, but never hit them. Each time the Parkers ducked and huddled, protecting their heads and faces.

"It's almost as if it's saying, 'Please don't hurt my baby,'" Mom acknowledged.

The Parkers tried to scoot along the path, but the distressed baby stayed on the trail, scurrying ahead of them.

After another attack on the Parkers, the mother bluebird again retreated to the juniper tree. Finally the baby bird hopped off the trail. Morgan, James, Mom, and Dad ran past until they were all at a safe distance.

When the Parkers were far enough away, they stopped and looked back. The adult bird was still in the tree, but the baby was now out of sight.

"Well, that was a first," Mom said while catching her breath.

"The baby sure seemed scared," Morgan said.

"Maybe it was hungry," James mused. "Its mouth was always open."

"And the mom," Dad added. "So powdery blue."

After a while the Parkers reached a sign marking a short side trail to several backcountry campsites.

The Parkers took the path to CP3. Nestled against a large boulder was a flat, juniper-shaded site, right in the middle of Chesler Park.

The Parkers shed their packs and began preparing lunch.

The family lounged in the shade much of the day—Dad reading, Mom sketching, and the twins writing. Later, as the sun began to dip below the rocky spires, the air seemed to take a nice cool breath. Dad stirred the chili for dinner and said, "It doesn't get any better than this, does it?"

Lucky Us

Just after sunset the Parkers began putting away their supplies from dinner.

Mom paused to gaze at the last splashes of light spraying across the grasslands and the fading pinkish hue on the towering pinnacles.

A tan-colored animal ran swiftly toward the middle of the park. "Hey, everyone, look," Mom whispered.

Morgan, James, and Dad came over to Mom.

The coyote bounded along, unaware of being observed.

Suddenly the animal stopped. It tilted its head up and began yipping.

Off in the distance another coyote answered the call. And soon still another joined in the chorus.

Eventually several coyotes trotted into view.

"The gathering of the clan," Dad announced.

The coyotes nuzzled up to each other and playfully pranced around. Then suddenly, the pack froze, staring across Chesler Park.

"They see something," Mom realized.

Morgan, James, Mom, and Dad scanned the grasslands framed by the circle of rocks behind them. Morgan was first to see movement, a glimpse of a larger animal with its tail flicking behind it. "Look!" Morgan exclaimed while pointing it out.

The animal weaved slowly between the grasses. Meanwhile Mom pulled out binoculars and found the animal through the lenses. "It's a mountain lion, and it's dragging something," she whispered.

The cat dropped its cache to the ground and looked toward the Parkers.

"Oops, now we've done it," Mom said, gulping nervously.

The cougar flicked its tail back and forth.

Mom and Dad put their arms around the twins. The Parkers huddled close. "Just stay together," Mom coached, "and we'll be fine. It's a long way off."

"It already has its dinner anyway," James tried to reassure himself with a shaky voice. "Whatever it dropped in the grass."

The Parkers heard the coyotes again and turned back to look. Meanwhile the large cat picked up its catch and continued lugging it along. "It's a deer," Morgan said as the cat hauled its food several yards farther.

A moment later the cat dropped the deer and let out a high-pitched wail.

The family stood still, mesmerized by the eerie call. "That," Mom shuddered, "just gave me goose bumps."

Even though the cat was a good distance away, Mom and Dad guided the family back against the rocks. Dad picked up a large, thick stick and noticed several decent-size stones strewn about. He scooted several of them closer with his foot without taking his eyes off the cougar. "Something to throw at it if needed," Dad explained.

Suddenly the lion crouched down. The Parkers watched the coyotes and the mountain lion as they appeared to be sizing each other up across the field. Mom held onto James and Morgan. "We are very lucky to see you," she spoke softly to the large cat. "But please don't come any closer."

Morgan glanced up at Mom. "It's not after us though, is it?"

"No," Mom replied. "Still, we have to be careful around a carnivore that size."

"Have you ever seen a mountain lion before?" James inquired.

"Never in all my years of backpacking and hiking . . . ," Mom said with awe.

The cat continued to glare at the pack of coyotes.

Meanwhile a few of the coyotes began loping toward the cougar. In a moment, two approached the cat from one side, came up to its behind, and tried nipping at it.

The cat turned and chased the intruders off, just as two more coyotes attacked from the other side. The mountain lion sideswiped one coyote, sending it tumbling into the brush.

Soon the cat was circled by the barking and growling coyote pack. The cat continued to twirl and whirl, trying to ward off each assault.

The cougar wailed again, sending another chilling call across Chesler Park. Then it hissed and pounced onto a coyote, temporarily pinning it down.

Two coyotes attacked from the other side. The cougar whipped around, freeing the pinned coyote, who instantly chased after the cat again.

The cougar called out again, this time sounding more distressed. It crouched down and watched the four animals slowly close in on it. The cat snarled at them and swiped its paws at the air several times while staying close to the dead deer.

Finally it gave up, dashing away into the protection of some rocks. Immediately the coyote clan dove into the deer carcass and began tearing away small chunks of meat.

By then it was nearly dark.

Mom took a breath and looked at her family. "You two," she spoke directly to the twins, "are sleeping between Dad and me in the tent tonight."

"And it's time we head in there," Dad added. "I think our gory Animal Planet show is wrapping up."

"Before we do," Mom suggested, "we should all go to the bathroom while there is still some light. I'll take Morgan and you take James."

"You're right," Dad agreed. "I don't think any of us will want to get out of the tent tonight."

The two pairs each walked only as far as they had to from the campsite. A moment later they all met back by the tent. The Parkers quickly got inside and nestled, snug in their cocoon.

"Wow" was all James could think of saying.

"You can say that again," Morgan added.

"Wow," the family echoed.

Sanctuary in the Shade

As the bright morning light quickly warmed the area, the Parkers ate breakfast to the views of Chesler Park. Birds chirped and sang in the distance.

"Did you hear the coyotes last night?" Dad asked his tired family.

"How could we not?" James replied.

"But it is so nice and serene now," Mom reflected. "This place is so special, and what we witnessed last night is gone. Poof!"

"We hope," Dad replied.

After breakfast the family packed up and resumed their loop trail backpack.

Once they left CP3, the trail dropped down between some large boulders. Then stairs cut into the rocks led the family deep into a hidden underworld.

As the Parkers plummeted into the shadows, Dad announced, "As if we haven't already seen enough phenomenal scenery."

Soon the family was walking in the cool, shady chasm known as the Joint. Morgan reached out and

The Joint

touched the walls of the slot canyon as they tramped by.

"Now this is chilly," Mom announced. "It's got to be at least twenty degrees cooler in here."

"I feel like we just walked into a giant refrigerator," James added.

The trail continued, winding between canyon walls and boulders over thirty feet high. Only a few small spots of sun reached to the canyon floor where the Parkers walked.

They marched on, passing other joints, or fractures in the rocks, leading to side canyons that also beckoned exploration.

The trail dropped down even farther into a deeper, darker, more mysterious underworld. Morgan shivered, noticing a tiny bit of steam coming out of her mouth as she breathed.

A few small lizards crawling along the vertical canyon walls scampered away as the Parkers passed by.

At one point Dad stopped and surveyed the whole rocky underworld. "I think this is where *Journey to the Center of the Earth* was filmed," he jokingly announced.

The canyon bottom trail was now well over fifty feet deep. Soon it got even deeper. And cooler.

Morgan spontaneously called out, "Hey, everyone!"

"Hey, everyone!" the rock walls replied.

A notched tree stump propped against a rock helped lead the Parkers farther down. "What a mysterious place this is," Mom remarked. "Although it is kind of claustrophobic."

Cool breezes wafted against the family's faces. Shortly after, the narrow slot canyon opened up into a large, underground room.

There the Parkers observed a fantasyland of man-made rock cairns and stone piles.

Morgan, James, Mom, and Dad surveyed the pillars and tiny monuments of rock scattered about the area.

Dad gasped in awe. "There are hundreds of these things in here," he exclaimed. "I guess this is part of the experience in the Joint. Usually in national parks you have to leave things alone, just as they were created by nature."

The family milled around the cavernous room, inspecting the creations. "Here's a tiny one," James called out.

"Look at this one," Morgan shouted. Then she studied the precariously positioned display a little closer. "I wonder how long it will stay standing."

"It kind of looks like a little Balanced Rock," Mom added.

James found a miniature pile of rocks placed into a tiny, natural hole in a rock wall. "Look at this one," he whispered, to protect the fragile discovery from crashing down with his breath.

The family spent several more minutes wandering around and admiring the man-made rock piles. Morgan took a bunch of pictures. And Mom did a quick sketch of the display she nicknamed "Mini Balanced Rock."

Eventually the Parkers gathered together on a large, flat rock nearby. There Mom and Dad pulled out snacks, and the family sat down and ate.

"It's so nice to be out of the sun," Dad announced between bites of his crackers.

After finishing his snack, Dad yawned and stretched out. Then he laid his head back and propped it against his pack. "I really didn't sleep much last night," he mentioned.

"Who could?" Morgan commented.

"I wonder where the mountain lion went," James mused. "I couldn't stop thinking about it. I mean, if it didn't get to eat that deer, it had to have something."

"I think we're all thinking too much," Mom said. Then she too lay down.

Soon all four Parkers were stretched out on the rock—in the cool respite of the Joint. Moments later Dad began to snore. Shortly after that, they all were asleep.

Sometime later, James was the first to wake up. He checked his family and determined they were all still somewhere in dreamland. Then, quietly, James opened his pack and pulled out his story. He picked up his pen, gathered his thoughts, and began writing . . .

"Sir. This is James William Parker, reporting back from downriver."

"What can you tell me, Mr. Parker?"

"Well," James replied to Captain Powell. "It's apparently quite rough down there. It could be very difficult travel. The rapids and white water ahead might devastate us."

"How far did you go?"

"Not that far. But we did run into a Native American scout who told us of the conditions far below. We had to turn back, though, due to rocky terrain and a lack of supplies."

"Do you think we'll capsize?"

"Based on what we heard, possibly."

"How did you get back?"

"Climbing over rocks and through groves of willow and cottonwood trees. It wasn't easy. I am all scratched up myself. And it was a little spooky too. One of the guys climbed higher for a better vantage point and walked right up to an Indian ruin. Nearby was a cave with ancient faces painted on it. We took a look and felt like we were seeing ghosts."

"Did you see any signs of recent activity?"

"No, sir. But we did keep our eyes out."

"Thank you, Mr. Parker. By the way, did you say 'James William Parker'?"

"Yes, sir."

"Well that makes both of our initials JWP."

"I know, sir," James replied.

James paused, trying to think of what to write next. He glanced at his family and saw they were still napping.

Then James heard voices coming from somewhere in the slot canyon. First they were faint, but they quickly grew louder. Soon footsteps accompanied the voices.

James looked around the Joint. Then he saw the people. One by one they entered the chasm from the opposite direction his family had come in. James watched them step out of the sunshine and into the underworld while heading toward the resting Parker family.

Soon, eight people tramped toward the Parkers, passing the rock displays along the way.

When they were about halfway down, Morgan, Mom, and Dad also heard the commotion. They each sat up and watched the visitors approach.

Finally the group reached the Parkers.

"Hello," Mom greeted them.

"Pretty cool in here," one guy replied.

"Definitely," Dad agreed. "You're a big group; are you on a tour?"

The hikers were carrying bags and day packs. "We're river rafting guides," one said. "And this is our day off. We like to come in here when we get some free time."

"Did you hike all the way out today already?" James inquired. "It's so early."

"Actually, no. It's only a short walk from a four-wheel-drive road."

The Parkers looked confused.

"Do you have a map?" one of the guides asked.

James took his map out. A person in the group showed the family the nearby jeep road.

"I hadn't even noticed that," Dad admitted.

"We couldn't have taken it anyway," Mom said. "Our car doesn't have four-wheel drive."

"True," Dad admitted.

"Besides, the hike was worth it," Morgan added.

"Well," the guide said. "Do you mind if we join you up there on that rock?" He held up a bag. "We've got our lunches in here."

Piling on the Rocks

The eight young men and women of the river crew hoisted themselves up to where the Parkers were sitting. Quickly they unpacked their food. "Leftovers from our last trip," one of them said, holding up a bag of rolls.

"We might as well eat now too," Mom suggested, dishing out peanut butter sandwiches to her family.

Soon everyone was feasting. "Want some pudding?" asked one of the crew members, showing the Parkers a sack of small containers.

"Sure," James said, looking at his parents. "But our spoons are still dirty from dinner last night."

"I'll show you a little trick," the guide offered. He peeled the foil lid off the top of the container and folded it into a makeshift spoon. Then he dipped the lid into the pudding, scooped some out, and inhaled the savory dessert.

"That'll work!" Dad exclaimed.

The Parkers each took a container from the river runners.

"What's it like on the river here?" James asked curiously.

"Well, there are actually two rivers in the park," one of the women replied. "And they're both very different."

"They are?" James asked, puzzled. He looked at his map.

The woman came over and pointed. "Our company runs trips on the Colorado River, here. Once we get down the canyon, though, both the Green River and the Colorado join and flow into Cataract Canyon. From there it's a white-water thrill ride and very difficult. But the Colorado River is where most of the outfitters go."

"What about the Green River?" Morgan asked, knowing that's what her family was planning to do.

Another crew member offered his opinion on it. "The Green River's a totally different experience. Most people start out at Mineral Bottom, over here. From there it's about fifty mostly flat miles of incredible canoeing and scenery. And with fewer outfitters, it's much quieter than the Colorado."

"And there are trails and side canyons with surprises along the way," another added.

"Really?" James asked, remembering his story. "Are there any arches?"

"Oh, I'm sure there are. Some of this country is the most remote in the United States. So there may be areas with unknown arches. And the Maze, over here," the guide pointed to a different section of the map, "is totally wild and mostly trail-less. An amazing place."

"Wow!" Mom chimed in. "This area sure has a lot to offer."

"What's being a river runner like?" Morgan asked.

"Never a dull moment," another crew person replied. "We steer the boats, cook, clean, set up camp, tell stories, and make sure everyone is fed, safe, and having fun."

Morgan then asked. "What's your favorite place along the river?"

"That's a tough question. There are so many possibilities."

"The whole Green River's my favorite," a crew member answered. "It's so much more of a wilderness journey. And it's where John Wesley Powell traveled."

James looked at the guide, wondering what he knew about Powell.

"Can you give us an example of a great place we might experience once on the water?" Mom asked.

"Depends on how much time you have and what you're willing to do," the guide replied. "But let me think for a second."

All eight river guides pondered suggestions.

"Cross of the Buttes," one finally said.

"What about Turks Head?" another chimed in.

"Where do these names come from?" Dad asked.

"They are the official names found on topo maps," a crew person replied. "But John Wesley Powell named most of them on his original journey."

"Really?" James asked, intrigued.

Then a group member called out. "Tilted Park!"

"Yeah. Tilted Park," another chimed in.

"Definitely. Tilted Park," the crew person next to the Parkers agreed.

"Tilted Park?" James asked.

The river guide explained. "That's a place on the river in Cataract Canyon. All the rocks there are standing up at angles, which is where the area gets its name. That in and of itself is a pretty cool sight to see."

"Our tours camp on a sandbar and build a fire. We dance on the sand at night."

"And during the day . . . ," another guide chimed in. "We're right next to 'rapid number ten.' And that's the best part. We break out all the goodies—inflatable duckies, dolphins, and all kinds of blow-up pool toys. Everyone walks upstream and plunges into the water to ride rapid number ten over and over."

"Some people do it all day long."

"And the water's so nice and warm." The guides kept taking turns filling in the details.

"That sure sounds like fun," Mom admitted. "You've got us thinking."

After the crew told of their adventures on the rivers, several of them wandered around the chasm inspecting the rock art. "I always feel it's like a religious shrine or temple in here," one commented in awe.

"Hey, check this one," another called out. "The rocks are stacked in this tiny hole in the rock wall."

Morgan and James jumped over to take another look at the now familiar miniature pile. All four of them began to walk around and admire the displays.

Then one of the crew members got an idea. "Do you want to help us make our own?"

Morgan and James both enthusiastically nodded. Quickly they each scanned the rocky underworld for any unused stones.

Morgan found several nearby. James grabbed a couple that were behind him. The two river runners dashed back to the lunch spot and hauled over a couple of larger rocks for the base of their stack.

"Let's start with this one," the guy said, holding up the biggest, flattest rock found so far.

"Okay," James replied. "By the way, I'm James and this is my sister, Morgan."

"I'm Matt and this is Carrie."

The four partners shook hands.

Matt placed the large rock at the bottom. James carefully added one on top of that. Morgan and Carrie also placed rocks on the growing pile. Then Carrie started a second pile near the first. All four kept adding more rocks and stacking them up. James found a bulkier one midway and held it in place until it felt secure enough to let go.

Soon there were two parallel growing stacks, teetering at times, but staying upright.

A moment later Matt and Carrie hauled over a larger, mostly flat rock and bridged it across the top, connecting the two pillars. By now

Mom and Dad and the whole river crew were the audience to the growing statue.

"Don't let go!" one person warned. "Or else the whole thing could come crashing down."

One by one, first Carrie, then Morgan, then James did let go. That left only Matt holding up the improbable arch creation.

Matt smiled at the audience. "Put some here and here on these little flat spots," he gestured to the twins and Carrie. "Smaller stacks for decoration before I let go."

Morgan, James, and Carrie followed Matt's prompt. They each made mini piles inside, on top of, and on overhanging shelves of their rock pillar.

"Whoo-hoo!" James exclaimed, as he finished his little addition on the very top of the pile.

"We made another Delicate Arch!" Morgan called out proudly.

"Well, sort of."

When all appeared ready, Matt lifted his hand slowly so that just the tips of his fingers supported the modern Stonehenge.

"Okay, everyone!" he called out.

"No. Wait!" Morgan stopped Matt. "Can I get a few pictures first?"

Morgan snapped some photos of Matt still barely supporting their structure. Then Mom came over. "You and James get in there. And you too," she said to Carrie.

Mom took a photo of all four artists, and then another of all the river runners surrounding the creation.

Then, finally, came the moment of truth. Matt again slowly lifted his fingers. "Hold your breath, everyone," Matt whispered. "No sneezing or coughing," he playfully added.

Everyone in the Joint was silent. Finally, Matt gingerly peeled away his fingers.

And the statue stayed put. Matt carefully tiptoed away then silently gave Morgan, James, and Carrie high-fives.

"We did it," Morgan whispered. "I hope it lasts."

"So we can see it when we come back," James said quietly.

"Whenever that might be," Dad added.

Finally it was time for the Parkers to go. They gathered up their gear and said good-bye to the river crew. James and Morgan hugged Carrie and Matt.

"Think about it. Get on the river," Matt called out as the Parkers began trudging toward the Joint's exit.

"Actually, we are already planning to," Mom replied. "We were just picking your brains for a preview."

Morgan, James, Mom, and Dad followed the trail and walked past more rock statues toward a slot between large rock fins. At the end of the slot, Dad shook his head and said, "What a place!"

Finally the Parkers stepped up between the rock walls and reentered the world of sunshine. They turned around and waved to the river runners one last time. Then the family began their journey back to the car.

The End and the Beginning

After the trail broke out into the sun, the family walked along quietly. At some point Dad glanced at his watch. "Whoa! It's 3:00 p.m.," he declared. "We were in there for quite a while. I think I lost track of time."

"We better get a move on then," Mom urged.

Soon the Parkers were on the jeep road. They passed a small parking lot with two four-wheel-drive trucks in it. "Those must be their cars," James said.

A short while later the trail veered off the road. The Parkers began climbing up through a series of rocky areas with cairns marking their path.

At one point Dad stopped. He looked around on the slickrock for where to go next. James, Morgan, and Mom caught up to him, and the family searched the area. Morgan saw the trail marker high above them.

"Up there," she pointed.

Dad looked up, then at the twins. "You two go first," he said. "I seem to keep losing the trail."

Morgan and James took over in front. "Come on," Morgan called back, climbing up the escarpment.

The twins continued to hike along, pausing at various intervals to find the pathway among the rocks.

"This way," Morgan guided.

"There's the trail," James observed later.

"Good eyes, you two," Dad encouraged.

"You're explorers, just like John Wesley Powell," Mom said at one point. "You've got it down."

James smiled at Mom's comment as he led the way up through another rocky area.

Finally, after a series of climbs, the path weaved between two huge rock fins. They entered a large, round valley surrounded by towering pinnacles of rock. "We're in Chesler Park again!" Morgan realized.

James verified the spot on his map.

The Parkers gathered together, gazing at the awe-inspiring place. "Let's stay close together in here," Mom suggested, remembering the carnivores of yesterday.

Soon the trail came to the original junction into Chesler Park. "We've come full circle now," Dad announced.

Morgan, James, Mom, and Dad turned to take in the scene once more. "Good-bye, Chesler Park," Morgan called out.

"We'll be back," James added somberly.

The family walked the last 2.9 miles back to their car briskly. At one point Mom announced, "That was a very magical place. A once-in-a-lifetime trail not to be missed. It was hard hiking at times and a long trail, but absolutely worth it."

"I agree," James echoed.

"Me too," Morgan added.

"You all know how I feel," Dad chimed in from the back.

Eventually Morgan and James led their parents down the final set of rock stairs to their waiting car. They loaded their gear and piled in, and Mom carefully drove the three-mile dirt road back to the campground.

The Parkers found an empty site nestled among the rocks at Squaw Flat Campground. They quickly set up camp, filled up on water, and began preparing dinner.

After dinner, Morgan pulled out her journal.

Dear Diary:

It's very hard ending this trip. But in many ways, really, it's just the beginning. Tomorrow we take off down the river.

Right now, though, it is sunset at Squaw Flat Campground in Canyonlands, and everything is quiet in this remote place. I can even see a small arch in some rocks across the way. James looked it up on his map. Wooden Shoe Arch is what this one is called.

It's very hard to come up with a top ten list for Arches and Canyonlands. It feels like we've been to a bunch of national parks over the last week or so.

So James and I collaborated and came up with a list together (sorry if it's a little long). But if you ever come out here, you'll see why:

Arches National Park

Delicate Arch
Landscape Arch
Surprise Arch in the Fiery Furnace
Crawl Through Arch in the Fiery Furnace
Climbing the rocks at Arches campground
Park Avenue Trail
Balanced Rock
The Windows and Double Arch
Rattlesnake, coyote, and rabbits at Arches
Broken Arch Trail
Tapestry Arch

Canyonlands National Park

Grand View Point

White Rim overlook

Aztec Butte views and granary

Upheaval Dome

The Neck overlook

Chesler Park

The Joint

Cave Spring Trail

Mesa Arch

Squaw Flat Campground, where we are now

Whale Rock

Believe me, the list could go on and on. And what if we went to the Maze? Or Horseshoe Canyon and the petroglyphs?

Next time?

James and I agree, there will definitely be a next time.

Signing off from southeast Utah,
Morgan Parker

The next day the family got up well before the crack of dawn. They quickly packed up and loaded everything into the car.

Mom and Dad took turns driving the two hours back to Moab.

The family found the river outfitters and checked in. Soon they were being shuttled back toward the Island in the Sky district of Canyonlands. But just before they entered the park, the driver turned off onto a dirt road that eventually led to the Green River.

At one point the road became quite steep. The driver turned toward the Parkers. "Hang on," he announced, grinning.

They wound down a series of very tight switchbacks with abrupt drop-offs.

Morgan, James, Mom, and Dad leaned toward the middle of the truck. They held their breaths on a few turns but soon breathed easier as the pitch of the road began to ease.

A short while later they reached their destination. As they neared the water the driver announced, "Welcome to the Green River!"

A Bureau of Land Management volunteer greeted the family and helped the Parkers unload their gear and carry everything to the water.

Morgan, James, Mom, and Dad stowed everything safely into their boats and put on life jackets. Then the volunteer asked them some questions.

"How much water do you have?"

Mom pointed out their gallon containers.

"And you have a week's worth of food?"

"Check," Dad replied.

"Sleeping bags?"

"Right over there," James said.

"Permits?"

"In here," Morgan pointed to a pack.

"Warm clothes?"

"Yep."

"Waterproof containers?"

"Yes."

"Map and compass?"

"In those."

"Flashlights and extra batteries?"

"In these."

"First-aid supplies?"

"In our packs."

"A topo map?"

"Right here," James said, patting his pack.

Finally, the outfitters steadied the boats while Mom and James got into one and Morgan and Dad climbed into the other.

"You all know to meet at Spanish Bottom, just beyond the Confluence, in four days, right?"

"We'll be there," Dad assured the BLM volunteer.

And with that they were shoved into the water.

• • •

At first the Parkers let the gentle current glide them along. They gazed at the rocky, tree-lined canyon that would be their home for the journey. Morgan looked back, watching the people on shore gradually appear smaller and smaller.

A great blue heron suddenly emerged from the trees and sailed into the sky. "Look at that!" Mom exclaimed as the bird flew high above the Parkers.

After a while they all began slowly paddling. James used only his left arm, still mimicking John Wesley Powell, while trying to guide his boat along. Around noon the Parkers pulled over at the side of the river for lunch. Afterwards, Morgan and James walked toward one boat, and Mom and Dad the other.

"Is that okay?" Morgan asked while climbing in.

Mom gazed downstream and smiled. "I think so."

On the third day on the water, in midafternoon, the rhythm of the journey took over, and James drifted into his imagination. After playing the next part of his story out in his mind, James grabbed his journal and started writing.

"Sir. I've already surveyed around the next few bends," James William Parker reported to Captain Powell.

"And it's safe for passing?"

"You bet," Parker replied. "At least until we reach the Colorado River. Beyond that is where the going gets rough."

"Thank you," Powell said. "Your information has been most valuable."

"At your service," the younger JWP replied. "Can I tell you what we saw down there?"

"Of course," Powell responded while gazing at the scenery.

James continued to write, pretending to tell Powell and the crew the information he and his family had discovered . . .

"It must have been quite a civilization that lived out here, sir," Parker said.

Powell stared off toward the horizon. "What else have you noted?"

"Lots," Parker reported. "We've seen several granaries now."

James paused for a second to gather his thoughts.

"And even some more paintings etched onto the rock. Petroglyphs. Figures of animals, snakes, hands, spirals, ladders, and faces. All very interesting."

"I see," Powell murmured. "Anything else?"

"Well, I want to go up on that rocky tableland and take a look," Parker suggested.

"Where to exactly?"

"The red rock up there looks level on top, and it is in that type of terrain that I think there might be more signs of ancient life."

"I think I'll go with you," Powell replied.

The two spoke of their plans to the rest of the crew. "One boat should wait here. The other should go downstream to near the end of that tableland. That way we'll have two paths back to you," Powell instructed.

After packing a small amount of supplies, James William Parker and John Wesley Powell bushwhacked past some willow trees along the river. Then they hiked up a side canyon and made a final climb to their destination a short while later.

The red tableland above stretched out a good distance. It was mostly flat but adorned with thousands of tiny, splintered rocks.

The two explorers scoured the terrain. After looking around, Powell and Parker both walked to the edge of the plateau to see if their crew was still visible. "I wouldn't want to get left behind up here," Powell mentioned, feeling some sense of the ancient inhabitants.

They both gazed down and immediately spotted one of their boats far below, drifting along on the water.

Meanwhile Parker began searching for signs of human life. Then he absentmindedly bent down and scooped up a handful of the thousands of tiny pieces of stone that littered the natural rock bench.

Parker took a moment to sift through the rock debris. He noticed several of the small stones had sharp edges and splintered sections. They didn't look natural. Parker's heart started to pound.

"Mr. Powell," Parker whispered, "I think we're walking on something very precious."

Parker showed Powell some of the small stones, pointing out the human-like cuttings on many of the pieces. "They look chipped off or fractured," Parker reported.

Powell scooped up his own handful and sifted through them. Then, slowly, his eyes lit up. He gulped before voicing his thoughts. "These rocks were chipped off to make arrowheads!" he realized. Powell noticed all the rock debris in both directions. "We're standing on an arrowhead-making factory! And this is what's left of it."

Both explorers gasped at the immenseness of their discovery. Powell picked up another pile. "Lithic debitage."

James had the captain say the words he remembered sharing with his class during his earlier report: *lithic*, relating to stone or rock, and *debitage*, referring to sharp-edged waste material.

The two explorers voraciously inspected as much debris as they could, then pocketed a small amount to show the crew and hopefully safeguard for a future museum.

James paused from writing for a moment. He looked up and noticed a red peninsula, a tableland, paralleling the river from above.

James smiled. There's one like the one I'm writing about, he told himself. I wonder if there are artifacts up there. And what about ruins and petroglyphs?

Suddenly James got hit with a blast of water.

"Hey!" James replied. "Watch out for my story."

Morgan splashed James again and again. "Aren't you going to paddle?" Morgan complained playfully.

James threw his journal and pen into a waterproof plastic bag and sealed it. He splashed Morgan back, then began paddling with both arms.

The twins paddled faster until they caught up with their parents, who were surveying the cliffs above. Both Morgan and James readied themselves to splash Mom and Dad when . . .

James spontaneously called out. "Hey, I've got a name for that arch!"

"The one in the story?" Dad asked.

"Yeah."

"What is it?"

"Arrowhead Arch."

"Why that name? Does it look like one?"

"It did, at least in my imagination," James replied, knowing there was a lot more to it than that.

This stamp, issued in 1969, honors the one hundredth anniversary of John Wesley Powell exploring the Colorado River.